Olympic Vista Chronicles

Yesterday's Gone

Book One

Kelly Pawlik

For permission, please email
olympicvistapublishing@gmail.com
Website: olympicvistapublishing.com

Bookstores and wholesale orders can be placed through
olympicvistapublishing@gmail.com

Cover art design: Greta Paliulyte

Pawlik, Kelly, author
Issued in print and electronic formats
ISBN 978-1-7777181-2-1 (paperback)
ISBN 978-1-7777181-1-4 (epub)

DISCLAIMER
This is a work of fiction. Any names and characters are used fictitiously or are the product of the author's imagination. Any resemblance to actual persons, living or dead, is entirely coincidental.

OLYMPIC VISTA
PUBLISHING

This book is dedicated
to Adelaide and Darius.
You may not be flesh and bone,
but my adventures with you are real.

One

Darius grinned out the car window. His family had moved from Boston to Washington State the day before. The small town of Olympic Vista was built up around a research and development facility referred to as The Link.

Darius and his twin sister, Davia, drove down the town's main street with their father in a shiny black sedan. Darius sat in the back, while Davia sat in her usual position of prominence in the front.

Olympic Vista was a smaller town than the twelve-year-old twins were used to. Davia crinkled her nose as she watched the scenery unfold outside her window. She grimaced as the stench of manure wafted in from the farms outside of town. She sighed when she saw the tiny brick mall and noticed the marked lack of buses and taxis.

Darius loved what he saw. He smiled as they drove by the quaint mall and marvelled at how many children rode around on bikes. Darius had read his share of novels and he knew this tiny town must have a mystery that needed to be unravelled.

Their father navigated the car out of the small downtown core along a meandering road dotted with small homes. He pulled into the small parking lot of a corner store at the intersection of a four-way stop. The lot was large enough to hold half a dozen cars, but was currently devoid of other vehicles. The pavement was uneven and there were no markings to denote parking stalls.

The store itself was a sad-looking single-floor building with stained white siding and bright yellow signage with red letters that spelled "Rutledge's Grocery Store." The building's shingled roof was speckled with clumps of green moss. One half of the storefront was lined with a two-tier wooden bench that held white buckets filled with bouquets of pink, red and yellow carnations.

"Eww," Davia muttered as she took in the store.

There was a "Loading Zone" sign with rusty edges affixed to the right-hand side of the store, next to a small makeshift loading bay. This section of the building was obviously a later addition and was set back a few feet from the main storefront. A wide set of sturdy wooden steps led up to an unmarked wooden door.

Three boys, maybe a year or two older than the twins, gathered at the side of the store in the loading bay. As the family stepped out of the car, they could hear the boys arguing. Darius noticed three bikes discarded on the ground a few feet from the trio.

"Don't be such a chicken! It's just a house," a boy in a black shirt scoffed. He took a long pull on his carton of chocolate milk.

The second boy was identical to the first, except he was in a blue shirt. He wiped his mouth with his arm and squished his milk carton with his other hand.

"Then you two do it!" a third, shorter boy retorted.

"The place is haunted. No way I'm going in," the blue-shirted boy chuckled.

"Besides, it's *your* dare," the black-shirted boy growled at the shorter one. He took another pull of his chocolate milk and turned to look at the newcomers. His eyes flicked from Darius to Davia, then turned back to his companions. "You could have picked truth and you didn't, Dillon."

"I'm not doing it. Give me a different one," Dillon demanded.

The blue-shirted boy tossed his squished, empty chocolate milk carton on the ground. He glanced up and saw Darius' father watching him.

Darius' father, Drew Belcouer, was an average man in many ways. He stood at about five foot seven inches tall and had short, dark hair. On this particular day he was dressed in chinos and a polo shirt. His eyes, however, were not average. They were cold and angry. He had a sour look about him, as though he'd smelled something unpleasant in the air that no one else could sense.

The boy in the blue shirt looked away from Darius' father and scooped his bike off the ground. He glanced at the crumpled milk carton, but left it on the pavement. "Then you're out. Let's bounce, Bru."

Without another look back, the identical twins biked away. Only the shorter boy, Dillon, remained in the small parking lot of the corner store with Darius and his family.

Drew strode toward the entrance. Davia trailed behind him. Darius ran his fingers through his brown hair and followed them.

Drew opened the glass door to the shop, and a small bell dinged in response. He held the door open and ushered Davia into the store. Darius' steps faltered as he crossed the parking lot. He paused and looked back at Dillon, who was picking up his bike.

"A haunted house?" Darius asked.

Dillon turned and scowled at him. Darius watched as the boy looked him up and down.

"Is there really a haunted house? Tell me where it is." Darius knew his father was waiting at the door, but his curiosity had gotten the better of him.

Dillon's scowl deepened. "It's the boarded-up one on Hyacinth Street." He turned away, righted his bike and pedaled off down the road in the opposite direction of the other boys.

"Darius," his father called from the doorway.

Darius hurried into the store. His father sighed impatiently as he followed him. The bell above the door jingled again as it closed.

A freezer purred loudly near the entrance. The store smelled of must and newspapers. Rows of metal shelves were packed with potato chips, cans of soup, boxes of crackers, sticks of deodorant, packs of batteries and everything in between. Behind the counter a teenager slouched on a stool. His head lolled to the side and his long hair obscured half of his face, which was dotted with acne.

Darius caught a glimpse of two boys and a girl, about his age, by the display of milk, soda and juice in the refrigerated section at the back of the store. The girl glanced at Darius as the trio moved toward a door marked "Employees Only." She had long, dark hair and the most solemn face he had ever seen. She was pretty, but in a strange way. He fought the urge to follow them as they opened the door and stepped into the back room. The door closed behind them.

"Pick out something you want," his father said as he moved to the newspaper stand. Darius pulled his eyes from the door. The teenager behind the counter jerked upright. Darius was sure he'd been asleep. Darius glanced about the store and his eyes settled on the freezer. He stepped toward it and wondered if the store carried ice cream sandwiches.

"Not ice cream," his father said without looking in his direction. "It'll ruin the upholstery."

Darius sighed. The upholstery was leather and could be wiped down, and Darius was sure he'd eat the whole ice cream before he got in the car anyway.

"Hurry up, Darius. I haven't got all day," Drew said as he placed a newspaper on the counter. Darius walked to the chocolate bar display and selected a Mars bar. He glanced toward the back room, but there was no sign of the three kids. He walked to the counter and placed his chocolate bar next to the newspaper. Next to the feature article, "Pine Park Reopens," was a small article titled "Morrison Allays Fears at The Link."

"Davia?" Drew called.

"What are people afraid of at The Link?" Darius asked the cashier, pointing at the paper.

The cashier shrugged.

Davia dropped a bag of assorted penny candies on the counter and Darius grimaced. As much as he enjoyed them, he hated how Davia sounded when she ate sour keys.

The pimple-faced cashier rung up their order without a word.

"Don't get any chocolate on the upholstery, Darius," Drew warned as they walked back to the car.

***

Tetsu led Adelaide and Kurt through the door marked "Employees Only." The back room of Rutledge's was dim. A single bulb leaked a sick yellow light over the excess goods stacked on the wooden floor. There was a big cardboard box labelled "Lay's," several cases of assorted soda, and all manner of other boxes and crates.

"We shouldn't be back here," Kurt fretted as he glanced around the room.

"Then look faster, Kurt. It has to be here

somewhere," Tetsu pointed out.

"It doesn't have to be here," Kurt argued. "They could have sold out already."

"This fast? Fat chance. They're hiding them," Tetsu spat. He peered into the recesses of a deep shelving unit.

Adelaide looked around. "There." She pointed at a stack of newspapers next to a side door that opened onto the alley. "Don't they get rid of those?"

"Yeah, they'll get picked up tomorrow," Kurt agreed.

The three of them set to work rifling through the day-old papers. While Adelaide searched the pile, she thought of the family who had come into the store. She had never seen them around town before, and they weren't the kind of people she'd forget easily. It was too late in the summer for tourists, and Olympic Vista wasn't a popular destination for family vacations to begin with.

"I got nothin'!" Tetsu complained. He kicked the doorframe.

"I'm not finding anything either," Adelaide said as she reached the bottom of her pile. She tucked her long brown hair behind her ear.

"Got it! Someone is cheating the system," Kurt said. He pulled the latest issue of *Conan the Barbarian* out from between the sections of one of the newspapers.

"Gimme!" Tetsu snatched it. "Is there any more in there?" He held the comic close to his chest and craned his neck to watch Kurt.

"*Are* there," Kurt corrected him.

Tetsu rolled his eyes. "*Are* there any more, Kurt?"

Kurt held up a single issue each of *The Uncanny X-Men, Fantastic Four*, and *Detective Comics*.

"Come to Papa!" Tetsu grinned. He snatched them out of Kurt's hands. The sinister faces of Batman's Rogues Gallery sneered at the Dark Knight.

"These weren't even the ones you wanted," Kurt argued.

"We have what we came for," Adelaide said. "It's time to go."

***

The drive from Rutledge's was as quiet as the drive there. Drew had lived in Olympic Vista once, and the tour had been his suggestion. Despite that, he had provided little information on their new home.

"Can we use the pool when we get back?" Davia asked, breaking the silence.

"Yes, sure," Drew said with an ambivalent wave of his hand.

Davia's lips smacked as she chewed her sour keys in the front seat. Darius had the back seat to himself and made the most of the view out both rear windows. He had seen some pastoral farms on the outskirts of town, but this area was comprised of mediocre houses with mediocre gardens. There were mediocre cars in driveways and mediocre people in their yards and on the sidewalks. Darius felt there should be something more. It was *too* mediocre. He just had to look harder.

The shiny black Lincoln Town Car passed James Morrison Elementary School. Drew pointed at the sprawling one-storey beige building. The parking lot was empty, its metal yellow gates pulled closed. The grassy field was withered from the heat of the summer, but it wasn't as yellow as Darius might have imagined. He wondered if they watered it, or if it was the result of all the Washington rain he'd heard about.

"There, that's your school," Drew said.

"I don't understand why we can't go to private school, Daddy," Davia sighed. "Isn't there one in the city?"

"You're going here."

The school called to Darius. He craned his neck

and watched the building until it was out of sight. Davia slumped into her seat and sucked on a sour key like an infant might mollify itself on a pacifier. They carried on, back in the direction of the family estate. Darius noticed a street sign up ahead. Hyacinth Street.

"Dad! Turn here."

His father glanced at him in the rear-view mirror.

"This is a tour, right?" Darius pushed.

The car indicator clicked rhythmically. Drew turned the car onto Hyacinth —yet another mediocre street. The properties all looked similar. More mediocre gardens and mediocre houses. The whole town was mediocre.

Then Darius saw it. The yard was thick with weeds and dead grass. The paint peeled and flaked off the trim. The windows were boarded up. This was the house: a dilapidated eyesore. To Darius it shone like a new penny on the sidewalk.

"Eww." Davia slurped harder on her sour key.

Darius turned to look back at the house as they drove by.

"I'll buy you bikes, but I'm going to drive you to and from school," Drew told them.

"What about your work?" Darius asked. He knew his father's office was located in Olympia and would require a short commute.

"I'll drive you to and from school."

Darius nodded. Davia continued to mope in the front seat.

The rest of the drive was quiet, broken only by the intermittent smack of Davia's lips as she ate another sour key. Drew turned up their long driveway. The front of the property was fenced, but there was no gate. Darius looked out over the expansive green lawn and perfectly manicured gardens. It was a far cry from their townhouse in Boston. Then again, it was a far cry from most of the houses in this town, too.

Their property was on the outskirts of Olympic Vista, closer to Olympia. Behind their back fence was a sprawl of unused fields set to be developed, and on either side were estates like theirs, but with tall fences and metal gates. As they climbed out of the car, their mother, Miranda, came around the side of the house. She was a slight, well-groomed woman. Her blond hair was styled into loose waves and she wore a high-necked blouse and jeans.

"There's a slight problem, Drew," she apologized.

"What now?" Drew scowled toward the backyard.

"The pool, it isn't—"

"What about the pool?" Davia demanded as she slammed her door.

A slight frown crossed Miranda's face. Drew waved in his daughter's direction in much the same way a person might bat at a fly hovering around their head. He looked at Miranda expectantly.

"They won't have it up and running today. It needs time to heat up and for the chemicals to be... balanced?"

Drew sighed.

***

Laughter and playful screams echoed across the lake. The light sparkled on the water as Adelaide floated on her back and kicked her feet gently back and forth. She closed her eyes and turned her face up toward the sun. The air was still. Combined with the clear sky and warm sun, it was the perfect summer day, which was a rare feat for Olympic Vista.

She needed to be here today. Rico, her mother's latest boyfriend, was over. Adelaide hated being around Rico. She sighed in contentment as she stretched her limbs like a starfish and basked atop the water.

Her eyes snapped open as something wrapped

around her ankle. Adelaide tried to kick her leg free, but whatever it was held fast. She opened her mouth to call out, but only took in a mouthful of water as she was pulled below the surface.

Two

Adelaide flailed her arms as she was dragged below the surface. She choked on water as it filled her lungs. She noticed the sun sparkle across the surface of the lake above her. She kicked her legs hard and connected with something.

Adelaide twisted and turned, then pushed herself off of whatever held her. She shot to the surface and spluttered as her head emerged from the water.

"Tetsu! Not cool!" she called as she swam back to the shore. She pulled herself onto one of the large rocks along the lake's edge and clambered out of the water. Once she was safely on the bank, she turned and glared back toward the lake, where Tetsu was now treading water.

"I can't believe you kicked me!" Tetsu chuckled while he rubbed his shoulder. His short black hair, which usually resembled a hedgehog's bristles, was matted to his head.

Adelaide plunked down on her Care Bear towel, then laid back and closed her eyes. The sun, which was often absent in Olympic Vista, made the inside of her eyelids gold. She savoured the warmth on her face and allowed herself to become hypnotized by the rolling motes of black and gold.

The lake was busy now. They'd arrived early enough to get a prime spot on the secret bank. The area could fit about a dozen people and was popular with teenagers in the evening. During the day, preteens basked on the rocks, clambered down the embankment, or jumped off the small rocky outcropping. It was a well-kept secret, in part because adults never walked this far to swim. The other reason was that the bank could only be accessed by a short, narrow trail that cut through a copse of trees and descended steeply. It was the perfect spot, until your best friend pretended to be a lake monster and dragged you under.

"You okay?" Kurt asked as he climbed out of the water and sat beside Adelaide.

She recalled the time she'd seen some boys from school throw a cat into the lake. It had looked miserable and tiny, not unlike Kurt at times. Kurt was short for his age, and scrawny. Most of his well-worn clothing was a size too small, which created a comical effect Adelaide never commented on.

She shielded her eyes from the sun with one hand and looked at Kurt. His reddish-brown hair hung in his eyes. He lifted a hand to push it away, but it fell back into place. Water trickled down his face. He was dripping wet. While usually his clothes were too small, his swim trunks were the opposite: obvious castoffs from someone larger than he was. The too-big waist was pulled tight with a drawstring and double-knotted. This caused him to look scrawnier still.

"I'm okay, Kurt. You didn't have to get out on my account."

Tetsu scrambled up the rocks and out of the water.

"Want to pack it up? I'm hungry." He scooped up his towel.

That's the way it was with Tetsu. He didn't apologize, he just moved on. Adelaide and Kurt watched as Tetsu dried himself off. "It's on me," he said after a moment.

Kurt pulled on his blue t-shirt and the three of them shoved their belongings into their backpacks. They slipped their flip-flops onto their feet, climbed the short ascent to the trail, and hopped on their bikes.

Douglas fir and Garry oaks shaded the bark-mulch path and provided a reprieve from the hot sun and the cacophony of noise from the lake. The three of them pedaled along the trail toward the main beach and the concession stand. The smell of fried food wafted in their direction as they drew closer.

Kids of all ages splashed and swam in the lake. Parents with big hats and striped umbrellas basked on colourful beach towels and blankets. Half a dozen people waited in line at the small stone building with its big window and display of condiments.

Tetsu dropped his bike on a patch of grass, adjusted his backpack strap and joined the line. Adelaide and Kurt set their bikes into the bike rack some twenty feet away. Kurt went back, picked up Tetsu's fallen bike and started to walk it toward the bike rack. Adelaide flanked the bike and took the other handlebar. Kurt let go as she rolled it into the rack next to their bikes.

"If he's not careful it'll get stolen," Kurt fretted.

"I know, Kurt," Adelaide agreed.

Adelaide's eyes fell on the angry man she'd seen at Rutledge's earlier. The boy was next to him, as were the girl and a pretty blond woman Adelaide assumed was their mother. They all sat on a large, pristine blanket. The boy glanced over and caught Adelaide's gaze.

"Where did Tetsu get the money for the concession?" Kurt asked incredulously.

"Beats me," Adelaide said, looking back at Kurt. "His parents? Maybe birthday money?"

The pair joined Tetsu in line and Adelaide stole a glance back at the beach. The boy on the blanket grinned at her. She averted her gaze and looked at the ground. It was the last day of summer break and she wanted to savour it. Tomorrow was the first day of their last year of elementary school. She knew everything was about to change.

"Burgers and sodas all around?" Tetsu asked as he reached the window. Adelaide and Kurt nodded.

Before long, the three of them sat on the grassy hill, which was dotted with patches of sand and led down to the beach. The sun beat down and the dry grass tickled Adelaide's legs. The bottom of Kurt's shirt was wet from his swim trunks. Adelaide had forgone putting on her shorts and t-shirt and wore just her faded blue swimsuit with her trademark black leather wrist cuff, which was studded with black and white squares. Tetsu wore just his swim trunks. Their backpacks, which were stuffed with their clothes and towels, lay scattered about them on the hill. Tetsu had shoved his change back into one of the pockets of his bag before he'd tossed it to the ground.

"This is the stuff," Tetsu said, his mouth full of

19

food. Adelaide watched as a big glob of ketchup fell out of his burger and landed on his bare chest. "It's a perfect day. *Conan*. Swimming. No school. Burgers. Soda. It doesn't get better than this. Am I right, Kurt?"

Adelaide nudged a distracted Kurt.

"What? Oh, yeah. Thanks, Tetsu."

"Just go ask her out," Tetsu said as he followed Kurt's gaze.

Adelaide didn't have to look. She knew Kurt was watching Farrah, who was busy giggling with her friends near the concession. There was a good chance Farrah would be Queen of the School this year. She was pretty and charming with big, blond hair like Farrah Fawcett. Adelaide liked her well enough, but she hated the sound of giggling. And all of them giggled.

"I can't. She'd laugh." Kurt sighed. "I should get more napkins." He scrambled to his feet and walked back to the concession. He was most of the way back, napkins in hand, when he froze in his tracks.

"Hey, shithead!" Jordan Kirkus called.

Adelaide frowned. Jordan led four boys in Kurt's direction. Kurt looked for an escape route.

"Yeah, you." Jordan pointed at Kurt. Jordan was tall with shaggy brown hair. He was a year older than they were. As of tomorrow, he was a high school student. Adelaide had suspected for a while that Jordan bullied Kurt, but Kurt had refused to admit it.

Adelaide stood up. "Leave him alone," she said as she raised herself to her full height and strode over to stand next to Kurt. At five foot three, Adelaide wasn't quite as tall as Jordan, but she was at least an inch taller than his friends.

Jordan looked surprised, but recovered quickly. "Or what?" he sneered at Adelaide.

***

"Daddy, maybe we could—"

"No. We're not going in the water," Drew snapped.

Miranda looked at her husband. "Drew, they could just—"

"No," Drew cut her off. "Everyone can stay on the blanket." He adjusted his sunglasses and surveyed the lake-goers.

Darius looked around. Kids his age were covered in sand. They ran barefoot into the water and splashed and screamed and pushed each other. He wasn't sure what the point of their visit to the beach was if they weren't allowed to get wet.

"What's wrong with the lake, Dad?" Darius asked.

Drew swivelled his head and appraised Darius. There was a pregnant pause. "Nothing. I don't want sand in the car."

Darius opened his mouth to object, but noticed a familiar face by the concession. The girl from the corner store. The two boys she had been with were there too. One of them was talking animatedly to her while they waited in line.

Life in Boston had been far from perfect. Darius had never felt like he fit in. He wondered what it would be like to spend time with this girl and her friends. They looked like a motley crew of outcasts, the exact opposite of most of the kids from his school in Boston. He took a breath and moved to stand up.

"Sit on the blanket, Darius," Drew commanded.

Darius glanced back at the concession, but remained seated.

***

Adelaide kept Jordan's gaze. "Or, I'll make you." She wasn't actually sure how she'd make Jordan leave anyone alone. She thought of kicking him in the shin. She hoped if she did, Tetsu would back her up long enough for Kurt to run away.

There was a long moment of silence as Jordan appraised Adelaide. She'd moved herself in front of Kurt. She held her breath and fought the urge to pick at the cuticles on her fingers with her thumb.

Tetsu was on his feet now. He moved to stand at her side. She felt him tense, like a cat ready to pounce. There was a smear of red across his chest. Adelaide suspected he'd tried to clean up the ketchup with his hand.

"You're lucky your girlfriend is here," Jordan said as he turned to walk away.

"You wish you had a girlfriend, Jordan," Adelaide challenged. "Instead, you have to run away from a girl younger than you are." Her voice was even and devoid of emotion. Butterflies flapped in her stomach. She fought the urge to wipe her palms on her swimsuit. Her mom had told her once that bullies didn't like to get called out or shown up in front of their friends. She hoped this time her mom was right about something.

Jordan's friends chuckled. Adelaide breathed a sigh of relief. Her mother, it seemed, did know a little about high school boys.

"Shut up!" Jordan called as he stormed toward the lake. The other boys followed, but Adelaide could hear their taunts and jeers.

"Thanks, Adelaide." Kurt let out the breath he'd been holding.

"No problem, Kurt," Adelaide said. She gathered up their garbage and tossed it in a nearby bin.

"You didn't have to imply you're my girlfriend, though."

Adelaide shrugged. "Let's get out of here." She wondered if Andy Katillion, the boy up the street, would still be mowing the lawn. She noticed more ketchup on Tetsu's hand, but said, "Oh, Tetsu, you have ketchup in your ear."

"What?" Tetsu said as he reached up, smearing ketchup from his fingers onto his ear. He raised an eyebrow at Adelaide. "Really?"

"I can't believe you fell for that," Kurt said with a laugh. "Nice one, Adelaide!"

"That's for pulling me under at the lake," she said in her monotone voice. There was a hint of a smile on her lips as she pulled her blue and white shorts over her swimsuit.

The three of them gathered their bags and bikes

and pedaled toward the parking lot. Adelaide could feel eyes on her. She wondered if it was Jordan, or the new kid with the angry father, or Farrah and her gaggle of gigglers. Either way, she was done at the lake.

Three

Darius craned his neck as his father pulled into a parking spot outside James Morrison Elementary School. Kids in bright colours filled the space that had been empty the day before. They stood in groups and regaled each other with tales from their summer vacations.

"I can't believe you expect me to go to school with six-year-olds, Daddy. I'm almost thirteen," Davia pouted.

Darius' lips twitched as he stifled a laugh. His sister was the only person he knew who would argue how mature she was while still using such a childish name for their father.

"Olympic Vista has an elementary school and a high school, Davia. You'll be at the high school next year. It's the way it is. And don't make me wait after school," Drew warned. "I have to get back to the office."

"Fine, Daddy," Davia said as she climbed out of the front seat.

"I won't," Darius added as he grabbed his backpack. He scanned the grounds as he closed the door. He grinned as he saw the trio of kids from the day before. The Asian boy—Darius thought maybe he was Japanese—snickered as Davia followed him onto the school grounds.

The girl turned and walked toward him. The boys followed. She was dressed in a denim skirt with a denim jacket over a pink shirt. Her brown hair hung long and loose, without any hair clips or hairspray. She wore a wide wrist cuff studded with black and white squares, which added an edge to her that he immediately liked.

The Asian boy wore a polo shirt tucked into a pair of beige slacks. His hair was cropped short, but it prickled out like a porcupine's spines. Darius watched him strut in his dress shoes as he followed the girl. The smallest of the three wore a faded yellow and brown striped shirt and ill-fitting jeans that looked worn at the knees. Darius could see the boy's off-white socks above his worn running shoes.

"Hello, I'm Adelaide. This is Kurt, and Tetsu," the girl said, as she gestured to each of the boys. Her voice was even, almost monotone, but enchanting. She had a small chin, a pleasant nose, and deep brown eyes that looked wise beyond her years.

"Are you a robot?" Davia asked before Darius could open his mouth. He wanted to kick her.

"No." Adelaide frowned. Her voice remained flat. Her brown eyes enchanted him. "That's a stupid question. I'm a person. With a few exceptions, robots have some sort of metal or plastic visible on their body."

"Are you calling me stupid?" Davia demanded.

Darius shifted uncomfortably. This was not how this had played out in his mind.

"No. I suggested your question was stupid," Adelaide said.

"Hey, um, hi," said Kurt. He was smaller than the others by far. His hair had a slight reddish hue and freckles dotted his fair complexion. He smiled at Darius, but turned to Davia. "I could introduce you to some of the younger kids if you want."

Darius willed himself not to laugh. People often found it hard to believe the two of them were twins. It wasn't just his light brown hair and her bright blond locks, or their very different demeanors. While Darius was about average height for his age, he stood six inches taller than his sister.

"Why would I want that?" Davia demanded.

"So that you can meet friends in your grade?" Kurt offered. His eyes shifted uncomfortably.

"I'm twelve," Davia said as she pulled herself to her

full height. "I'm not younger than my brother. And I'm *not* younger than you."

"Right, then," Adelaide said. She looked from Darius to Davia, and then back again. "Good luck this year." And then she turned and was gone. Kurt and Tetsu followed.

"Thanks a lot." Darius frowned. He decided not to remind Davia he was several minutes older than her.

"What? You don't want to hang out with those losers anyway. Look at them! Losers with a capital L. I mean, did you see that one boy's pants?"

Darius was grateful he and Davia had had to be placed in separate classes due to their late enrollment. When the bell rang, he navigated the halls to his classroom and away from his sister.

The cloakroom had a series of hooks, each with a small piece of laminated paper above it to denote whose it was. From the doorway he could see a message on the chalkboard: "Welcome, class!" Darius could just make out wooden shelves that ran underneath the windows down the length of the room, and an empty bulletin board ready to display students' projects.

He grinned when he saw Adelaide. She hadn't noticed him yet. The cloakroom was a flurry of activity as students found their hooks and hung up their backpacks. Shoes squeaked on the linoleum floor and dozens of backpacks were zipped and unzipped. Darius shoved his bag onto his labelled hook, draped his coat overtop, and beelined out of the cloakroom to an empty seat next to Adelaide. She glanced over and he thought he saw her eyes widen slightly.

"I'm Darius." He smiled.

"Okay," Adelaide said. She opened her mouth to say something else when Darius sensed someone come up behind him.

"You can't sit there," Tetsu said.

Darius turned.

"You can't sit there," Tetsu repeated.

"It's fine, Tetsu," Adelaide said. "You can sit here." She gestured at a seat on the other side of her. Tetsu grumbled as he sat down where she indicated. Kurt was just behind Tetsu, and he took a seat behind Adelaide. The room buzzed with chatter as students took their seats.

A girl with long blonde hair walked over and scowled at the desks. "Okay, I guess I'll just sit here," she said as she plunked into a seat next to Kurt. "I can't believe I'm not in a class with Julie this year. It's the worst!"

"I can see you're in a pleasant mood, Sophie,"

Tetsu teased.

Sophie turned and seemed to notice Darius for the first time. Her grimace turned to a smile as she ignored Tetsu and she batted her eyelashes at Darius. "You're new. Hi!"

A tall man with close-cropped grey facial hair and warm eyes stood up from his desk.

"Welcome, and hello, class!" he called.

"Hello, Mr. McKenzie!" some of the class responded. Some sounded enthusiastic. Others mumbled their response. Adelaide had a soft smile on her lips.

"Let's try that again," Mr. McKenzie smiled. "Hello, class!"

"Hello, Mr. McKenzie!" Darius joined in this time. Mr. McKenzie was a far cry from the stern teachers at Wiltshire Preparatory Academy. Darius had a good feeling about Olympic Vista.

When the recess bell rang, he followed Adelaide and her friends outside.

"Hi," he said with a grin.

"Hello." Adelaide appraised him.

"Is your sister joinin' us?" Tetsu eyed Darius with suspicion.

"Probably not." Darius turned back to Adelaide. "I

saw you guys at the corner store yesterday."

"Yeah?" Tetsu scoffed.

"Yeah, you guys went in the back."

Adelaide changed the subject. "So, what kind of stuff are you into?"

"Oh, um ..." Darius was surprised by the question, but answered it anyway. "I like to ride my bike, I guess. My dad's getting me a new bike today. And I like swimming. I like reading mystery novels, like the *Hardy Boys*. And I'm pretty into music—bunch of stuff you probably haven't heard of." Darius realized the words were falling out of his mouth faster than he wanted them to. Even worse, he sounded pretentious. He forced himself to take a breath. "We just moved out from Boston. My dad came here to expand the office."

"What's he do for work?" Tetsu interjected.

"I don't know," Darius answered truthfully. He hadn't ever taken much interest in his father's job. "He travels a bit. Lots of meetings. Sometimes he goes away suddenly. He doesn't talk much about work."

Tetsu appraised him. "Businessman. I get it."

"And this music I probably haven't heard of?" Adelaide asked. Darius wasn't sure, but he thought she was amused.

"Oh, Fleetwood Mac and The Clash. I mean, I'm into other stuff too. I like Elvis Costello and Cyndi Lauper. I like pretty much all of it. Except country. I don't like country music."

"But polka is okay?" Tetsu asked with a smirk.

"At least you can dance to it," Darius quipped. He was sure there was a hint of a smile on Adelaide's lips now. He breathed a sigh of relief.

"Hey, hi," the blond girl from class said as she walked up to the group. She nodded at the others and then smiled at him. "So, is your family rich?"

"Sophie," Kurt hissed. "You can't just ask that."

"Sure she can." Tetsu turned to Darius.

"I guess so," Darius said as he looked at his clothes and then at theirs. He recalled their worn bikes at the lake and thought of the new one his father would bring home for him today. He'd never thought about it before—everyone he knew in Boston had seemed like his family.

"Well, it's really nice to meet you, Darius. I'm Sophie. Sophie Katillion." She smiled again and moved closer to him.

"Nice to meet you," Darius offered. Sophie giggled.

Darius glanced over at Adelaide. She looked out toward the playground. "So, I heard this place is weird,"

33

he said. "Because of The Link."

Adelaide's gaze was still on the playground. Tetsu shrugged. Sophie flicked her hair over her shoulder and smiled.

"They do a lot of experiments there, I guess," Kurt said. "They say it doesn't affect us and there's a lot of safety protocols in place. Between you and me, though," Kurt said, leaning in, "it's full of commies. *They* are the real threat."

"Come on, Kurt," Sophie said as she rolled her eyes.

Kurt pursed his lips and looked at the ground. "That's what my dad says."

"No one believes that. And the other stuff is just rumours," Tetsu said. "Got nothin' to do with commies or Nazis. It's just some stupid science building and observatory."

"What about the haunted house?" Darius had thought about it nonstop since he'd heard about it yesterday. He wanted to ask Dillon or the twin boys more about it, but he hadn't seen them at the school. "Have you guys ever gone there?"

"What haunted house?" Adelaide's eyes flicked back to him.

"The one on Hyacinth Street. It isn't far from where

I live." Darius liked her eyes on him.

"That's a really nice area," Sophie cooed.

Darius shuffled a step away from Sophie. Unlike with Adelaide, he didn't like how she looked at him.

"I was going to check it out." Darius ran his hand through his hair, and looked back at Adelaide. "Tonight."

Adelaide cocked her head and looked at him. "I'm in."

Darius grinned.

***

The rec room in the Katillions' basement had faux wood panelling, orange shag carpet, and long narrow windows on opposite walls which let the smallest amount of light filter into the room. Two ceiling lights provided the room with a warm yellow glow. A brown- and cream-patterned couch sat along one wall, facing a long, low coffee table used for snacks, board games, homework, and a myriad of other purposes. Along another wall, a large backless wooden shelf, flanked by two large speakers, held a record player, a receiver and a cassette player. Assorted photos of the family were displayed in wooden picture frames next to the electronics.

Adelaide thumbed through the Katillions' record collection. *Out of Our Heads* spun on the record player. It wasn't her favourite Rolling Stones album, but she had put it on for Tetsu. She always enjoyed his rendition of "(I Can't Get No) Satisfaction."

Adelaide wasn't certain this year was off to a good start, but tonight's excursion would be a welcome distraction. Her mother had lost her job. Again. And her mother's current boyfriend, Rico, blinked too much. Almost no one noticed, but it made Adelaide uncomfortable.

Tetsu snatched a Rice Krispies treat off the white and gold Corelle plate on the coffee table. He flopped onto a beanbag chair and licked his lips in anticipation.

"I can't believe we're going to sneak out tonight," Sophie whispered.

"Who do you think can hear you down here?" Tetsu asked as he looked up from his snack. "And what happened to the whole 'I won't have time for you this year' thing?"

"Hush, you! What if there are rats and spiders?" Sophie asked.

"Probably are," Tetsu replied. He took a big bite of the Rice Krispies treat. "Might crawl up your legs." Bits of

Rice Krispies fell from his mouth.

"You're spitting," Adelaide said, her eyes still on The Beatles' *Rubber Soul* album.

"So?" Tetsu fired back.

"So, it's kind of gross," Sophie chimed in.

There was a knock at the door and it opened a second later.

"You can't just barge in!" Sophie yelled.

"Mom asked me to bring these down." Sophie's older brother, Andy, held up a plate of vegetables.

Adelaide's heart fluttered. She loved when Andy brought an extra snack down. She stole a glance at him. He was taller than most boys his age. His shaggy blond hair fell around his face like a worn halo. He had warm brown eyes and an even warmer smile.

"Just put them on the table, then," Sophie sighed.

"Can I have a Rice Krispies treat?" Andy asked. He was going through puberty and his voice squeaked.

"Can I have a Rice Krispies treat?" Sophie mocked. "You are such a mutant."

"How was school?" Adelaide looked up from The Beatles' White Album. It was her least favourite cover. "Your first day of high school, right?"

"Yeah, uh, yeah, it was." Andy smiled. He picked

up a Rice Krispies treat and sat down on the orange shag carpet near her. "It's different." His voice went up an octave.

"That makes sense." Adelaide could smell Old Spice and soap. Most of the boys she spent time with smelled like sweat and farts. She smiled. She could listen to Andy talk for hours.

"Get out of here! You are such a loser!" Sophie yelled. "Find your own friends."

Andy picked himself up off the floor. "See you guys."

Adelaide liked when Andy sat in the Hideout with them, but she worried if she spoke up, Sophie wouldn't invite her over anymore. She didn't want to go home. She glanced up to smile at Andy, but he'd already walked out the door.

Four

The room was dark. The faint sound of music filled the air. Adelaide reached over and hit the button on her alarm. The music turned off. Even the radio announcers weren't up at this hour. It was just after midnight and the house was still.

Adelaide climbed out of bed. Her feet were cold on the wooden floor as she changed out of her pyjamas into worn jeans and a dark sweatshirt.

She opened the door to her room and peered out. She was sure that Waylon, who rented a room upstairs and worked security for a bar in Olympia, was at work. The other room upstairs hadn't been rented out since the perky redhead left two months ago. Adelaide hated how that woman had patronized her, and she'd been relieved when the woman had moved in with a new boyfriend. Still, she wished her mother would rent the room back out. The cupboards tended to have more food in them when roommates paid rent.

Adelaide slipped out onto the landing. Across the

hall from her room was her mother's. Violet, another roommate, rented the room next to the staircase. Adelaide imagined Violet had already cried herself to sleep. Sometimes Adelaide would slip into Violet's room and stroke her hair until she fell into a fitful slumber.

Adelaide was sure her mother and Rico had tired themselves out for at least a time. She tiptoed into the hallway, careful to creep along the wall. The old wooden floorboards were notorious for how they creaked and shifted underfoot, but Adelaide knew the house better than anyone. She wondered if her mother had memorized every nook and cranny when she was younger. It was hard to imagine her mother's attention on anything for long.

Adelaide clung to the banister as she made her way down the edge of the wooden staircase. She crept to the front door, pulled on her runners and eased the door open.

She breathed a sigh of relief as she pulled the door closed behind her.

Then she turned and stiffened as a shadow on the porch moved toward her.

***

Darius pulled a black sweatshirt over his jeans. His heart pounded in his chest. He'd never snuck out of the house before, but there'd never been a mystery to solve before either. He eased the door to his bedroom open. The hallway was dark when he stepped into it and pulled his door closed behind him.

Darius jumped as his sister snuffled a snore across the hall. He exhaled slowly and padded down the hallway to the top of the staircase. The board on the top step creaked as he stepped on it. The sound seemed to echo through the otherwise still house. Darius sucked in his breath and waited. He couldn't hear anyone.

Darius marvelled at how many of the boards creaked. During the day the giant house seemed quieter. He wondered if Davia's sheer presence was so loud it could mute the house itself.

Darius reached the foyer closet, collected his shoes, and stole away into the night.

***

The houses were dark and bushes loomed like monsters on the front lawns as the kids made their way to

Hyacinth Street. Sophie and Tetsu had proper bike lights, but Adelaide had had to improvise, using duct tape to affix a flashlight to her handlebars. Kurt stayed close to her and Sophie so he could use their lights to navigate his way.

"I can't believe I scared you," Tetsu said as they pedaled down the dark and deserted street.

"You did it on purpose," Adelaide pointed out.

"I didn't think you should be alone. Always good to have a friend."

"Mm-hmm," Adelaide answered. Despite the initial scare, she'd been relieved to find Tetsu waiting on her porch. They biked on in silence for a few minutes.

"He's pretty cute, right?" Sophie asked, making reference to Darius.

"If you like rich kids, maybe," Tetsu scoffed.

"Adelaide?" Sophie asked.

"We should probably be quiet," Adelaide suggested. There was something different about Darius and it wasn't just how his Boston accent made him drop the "r" on some of his words. He made her excited and nervous all at once. The only person who'd made her feel like that before was Andy. Just the thought of Andy made butterflies flap in her stomach. She missed seeing him on the bus, even if he never sat with her. She wondered if

Andy had a girlfriend now that he was in high school.

They pedaled on in silence until Adelaide heard a sound in the distance.

"Get off the road now," she directed. She zipped her bike onto a nearby lawn and hid behind a giant rhododendron. She flicked off her flashlight and the others followed her lead.

"What are we—" Sophie started to ask.

Beams from a car's headlights illuminated the street. Adelaide put her finger to her lips and looked at Sophie. The four of them balanced their bikes and stood in silence as they waited for the car to pass.

"We aren't doing anything wrong," Sophie said after it passed by.

"No adult should be okay with four kids out in the middle of the night," Kurt said. "They'd call our parents, or the police."

They turned their lights back on, navigated their bikes off the lawn and pedaled on down the road. Sophie took the lead and Adelaide fell back to ride alongside Kurt, who had started to lag behind.

Sophie had changed over the summer. Like Adelaide, she'd grown in height. The two girls now stood several inches taller than Tetsu and Kurt, but Sophie had become consumed with whatever makeup, hairstyles and brand name clothing *Teen* magazine said were all the rage. The Friday before her last sports camp of the summer, Sophie had told them she wouldn't be able to spend as much time with them at school. When Kurt had asked why, Sophie had rolled her eyes. The answer went unspoken, but Adelaide knew it was because none of them were cool and Sophie needed to be popular this year.

Adelaide was disappointed Sophie had tagged along. She knew Sophie's physical prowess would be to their benefit, but it was clear she was interested in Darius. She shook her head, not certain why that bothered her.

It was another twenty minutes before they reached Hyacinth Street. They didn't encounter any more vehicles, but a noisy dog in someone's yard gave Kurt a scare.

Darius moved out from the shadows when they arrived. Adelaide could see his big grin in the light of the moon.

"Hi! You guys made it. Rad."

"Yeah, we said we'd be here," Tetsu asserted.

"Thanks for waiting," Adelaide said as she turned to survey the house. The windows were boarded up and the roof sagged. The grass was long and yellow from the summer weather. There was an overgrown garden under the large front window. Some of the pieces of plywood over the windows were covered in graffiti, but Adelaide couldn't quite make the words out in the moonlight. She turned back to the others. "So, we just ... go in?"

They all looked at each other, then wheeled their bikes to edge of the property and set them down. Adelaide noticed Darius glance at them before he set his bike on the yellow grass. She thought she could make out a kickstand on his bike. Adelaide peeled the tape off her flashlight, removed it from her bike, and stuffed it into her backpack.

For a long moment the five of them stood there, illuminated by the soft glow of the moon.

"This was already an adventure," Kurt pointed out. "I mean, we could just—"

"We're already here. I'm not afraid to go in," Tetsu boasted.

"All right, then," Darius replied. "Let's go."

"Kurt," Adelaide said. "If you don't want—"

Kurt moved first. He strode to the door and, after a second of hesitation, the others followed behind. Kurt reached out and grasped the handle. Then he turned it.

The door didn't budge. They all stood in silence for a moment. Sophie glanced at Darius. Darius frowned as he looked up at the upper windows. Adelaide tilted her head and listened.

Kurt fished into the pocket of his coat and pulled out a small screwdriver and a bobby pin.

"Why do you have those?" Sophie hissed in the dark.

"Why do you think?" Kurt bent the bobby pin and inserted it into the lock along with the screwdriver. He fussed with the lock for a few minutes before he grimaced. "I can't do it."

"It's okay, Kurt. We'll try the back. Come on," Adelaide said as she led the way around the property.

The backyard was as unkempt as the front. The grass was long and dead, paint peeled off the back fence, and even some of the boards over the windows had given up. Tetsu strode to a window where the plywood hung on by only a single nail. The rotten board could be moved like a pendulum. Only part of the glass behind it was covered.

Adelaide stepped up beside Tetsu and leaned in close to the glass. She could just make out lumps of furniture packed tight inside the room.

Tetsu reached out and tried to push the window up. The old paint adhered the window to its frame like glue. It held fast. Tetsu pulled his switchblade from his pocket and Adelaide stepped back as he cut an incision along the frame. He flicked the blade back in on itself and tucked it into his pocket again.

"Ready?" Tetsu asked.

"Ready!" Darius whispered as he came up behind them. "Here, let me help."

Adelaide held the plywood out of the way as Darius and Tetsu gritted their teeth and pushed the window up on its runners. It resisted for a moment before it slid up and banged against the top of the frame.

Everyone flinched.

"I'll go first," Darius said. He reached in and pulled himself up over the window frame, before he landed in the room with a faint thump.

"Me next," Adelaide said. Tetsu nodded and gave her a boost.

Adelaide's eyes adjusted to the room as she moved further in. She wrinkled her nose as dust particles tickled her nostrils. The room was musty with the faint odour of mothballs. Couches and shelves were pushed together. An old wooden coffee table stood on its end. There were several rolled-up rugs in one corner, and a collection of frames leaning against one of the walls. The only door was closed and there was no light under the door frame.

Sophie, who had followed Adelaide in, helped pull Kurt through the window. Darius was already at the door. He had one hand on the brass knob, and in his other was a sturdy flashlight.

As Tetsu climbed in the window, there was a thump from upstairs. He sucked in his breath.

"I hope it's a raccoon," Kurt murmured.

Tetsu exhaled. "How'd it get in?" he asked with false bravado.

"Let's find out," Darius said as he turned the handle and walked out into a dark hall.

The corridor was wide with a wooden floor. It was devoid of side tables, photos or paintings. Not even a runner lined the hallway.

"Stay close to the edges," Adelaide offered as she stepped out behind Darius. "They shouldn't creak as much." She pulled her flashlight out of her bag and clicked it on.

The beams from their flashlights cut through the dust that floated in the air. They moved from one empty room to another. As they reached the doorway to the kitchen, they heard another loud thump from upstairs.

Adelaide held her breath. There was a growl. Long and low. And another thump.

"Let's go see what it is," Darius whispered as he started for the stairs.

"I don't think that's the best idea," Kurt suggested.

"Don't be such a girl," Sophie said, but her voice quavered.

Darius moved closer to the stairs. Adelaide glanced at her friends. Tetsu nodded. They followed Darius to the staircase and crept up the wooden steps. They reached the landing when the sound of metal hitting metal made them freeze.

"Is that chains rattling?" Sophie hissed.

"Maybe," Adelaide offered.

They moved slower now, with Darius in the lead. The top of the stairs opened to another hallway with four doors, all closed. Darius moved to the first one, twisted the handle and pushed it open part of the way. The room was dark. He directed his beam of light into the room. It was empty.

One by one they looked in the other rooms. Tetsu's hand was on the last door when they heard another thump, followed by the sound of chains.

"It's coming from the attic," Darius declared as he moved the beam of light to the ceiling.

Tetsu pushed his door open to reveal an empty room.

"How do we get up there?" Sophie asked.

"There," Darius pointed at a small rope that hung from a trap door in the ceiling.

"Boost me up," Adelaide said. She'd come too far to turn around now. She looked at Darius.

"Oh, okay, are you sure?" Darius fumbled as he handed his flashlight to Kurt.

"Boost me up," she repeated. She looked at Tetsu and indicated he should help. The two boys crouched down. Adelaide steadied herself by grabbing their shoulders as she stepped onto their outstretched hands. Tetsu rose faster than Darius. Adelaide squeezed Darius' shoulder more tightly. "Easy," she warned. Both boys rose to their full height. Adelaide reached and grasped the rope.

"Got it." Adelaide held onto the rope as she jumped off their hands. Above her, the trapdoor opened, revealing the bottom of a retracted set of stairs.

There was another long, low growl, followed by a thump.

The five of them looked at each other. Tetsu pointed at himself, then Adelaide, and then upstairs. Adelaide nodded. She pointed at Darius and indicated he should follow them up. Tetsu fingered his switchblade.

Sophie, who was almost as tall as Adelaide, and

taller than any of the boys, reached up and pulled down the set of stairs from the trapdoor.

Without a word, Tetsu charged up into the attic. His feet were loud on the wooden steps. Adelaide followed him, and Darius tailed close behind her.

The room was dark. They cast their beams about.

A sudden thump made them all jump. Darius chuckled. Adelaide swivelled and saw a small engine illuminated by the beam of his flashlight. She shone her flashlight around the area.

There was a series of rods and reels affixed to the engine. A steel-toed boot was fastened to the handle of one of the reels. The three children watched as the reel turned and thumped the boot onto the wooden floor.

Darius traced another rod with the beam of his flashlight. A series of reels rotated at longer intervals than the ones that thumped the boot into the floor. These ones shook a chain that dangled from the sloped ceiling.

"This is so rad," Darius chuckled.

"Is everything okay up there?" Sophie hissed from the bottom of the steps.

"It's fine," Adelaide whispered back. "It's a contraption designed to make it seem like it's haunted. But what about—"

Adelaide was cut off as a long low growl echoed from below them.

"That. What about that?" she finished.

"The basement!" Kurt called in a raised whisper. "I bet it echoes through the vents!"

Darius, Adelaide and Tetsu climbed down the steps.

"The only room we haven't checked is the kitchen. There must be a door to the basement there," Darius said.

The group pushed the staircase and attic door back into place before making their way back downstairs toward the kitchen.

"There's probably a small generator down there as well. A quiet one. Maybe it's playing a cassette?" Kurt offered as they rounded the corner.

"Maybe," Sophie murmured. "But maybe we should just get out of here now."

There was a loud snap. Kurt sucked in his breath. Adelaide sensed the scream that started to rise in his throat. She clapped her hand over his mouth and moved her flashlight beam down toward his foot.

"It's a mouse trap. It's just a mouse trap." Her voice was low. She leaned in and made eye contact with Kurt. "You're okay."

Kurt's eyes were wide, but he nodded.

"I'll get it off you, okay? But you have to stay quiet." Adelaide searched his eyes before she removed her hand and bent down.

"Holy crap!" Tetsu whispered. "Did you see the look on Kurt's face?"

"Stop that," Darius said to Tetsu. "You okay, Kurt? Do you need help, Adelaide?"

"I've got it," Adelaide said as she pried the trap off Kurt's foot. She dropped it on the floor next to him. There was a faint imprint on Kurt's runner, but it was otherwise untouched. "Is your foot okay?"

Kurt nodded. His eyes were still wide.

"All right, then." Darius grinned. "I want to see the basement."

Adelaide felt his eyes on her and she looked over. She could see them shine, even in the dim light. His enthusiasm stirred something in her.

"I'm not ready to go, either. We should see what's in the basement," Adelaide declared.

Darius grinned wider and reached for the basement door. He twisted the handle. Adelaide sucked in a breath.

And then, thunderous in the otherwise still house, the phone rang.

Five

Tetsu reached over and clapped his hand over Kurt's mouth. The quintet gaped at each other, frozen to the spot in the dark kitchen.

The phone rang again.

Footfalls hammered up the basement stairs. Darius looked around the kitchen. Kurt scrambled to a lower cabinet, pulled open the door and climbed inside. Tetsu followed his lead and climbed into his own cupboard. Sophie glanced at them, but the footsteps were almost at the top of the stairs. She pushed herself into the furthest corner of the room. Adelaide was frozen to the spot. Darius grabbed her hand and pulled her under the sturdy wooden table next to the banquette.

"Flashlights," Darius hissed.

The room went dark as the phone rang a third time. The basement door slammed open and light filtered along the tile floor. The edges of it illuminated one of Adelaide's sneakers. She pulled her legs in and made herself as small as she could under the table.

Darius heard footfalls in the kitchen. A smell reminiscent of pickles wafted through the air.

"What?" a male voice demanded. There was a pause. "Bring what you can get." Another pause. "I need the material. It's fresh, right?" The man sighed. "Fine, bring them. I'm here. Just rap at the basement window."

Darius wanted to pull Adelaide in closer. He liked the way her shampoo smelled. He felt her shift as she pushed herself further away from the basement light and huddled against him. He'd let go of her hand as they crawled along the floor, but she took it again. It was soft and he squeezed it.

"Incompetent," the man huffed as he slammed the receiver down. He opened the fridge, and light illuminated more of the kitchen.

One of the cupboards was ajar. Darius wondered how well Sophie was hidden in the corner of the room. All the man had to do was turn around. They were trespassing: breaking and entering. If the man noticed any of them, Darius would have to tackle him. His body tensed, ready to spring into action.

The man closed the fridge. There was a small hiss and then a beer bottle cap clicked as it skipped along the kitchen counter. The man took a swig. The light from the basement was blocked as he stepped through the doorway and then closed the door.

Footsteps receded down the stairs, but the kitchen was still for several moments. Adelaide started when Sophie stepped out from the corner.

"We have to go. Now," Sophie urged in a loud whisper. She opened the cupboard Kurt was hiding in.

"No way, I want to know what he's doing in the basement," Tetsu whispered as he emerged from his own cupboard and turned his flashlight back on.

Darius squeezed Adelaide's hand again, then climbed out from under the table. He offered his hand to her again to help her up as she emerged. The light was dim, illuminated only by a few flashlight beams, but he thought her cheeks were touched with pink. She dropped his hand.

"It's dangerous!" Sophie insisted as she moved back to the hallway. "We'll get in trouble. Come on, Kurt."

Darius stepped toward the basement door. He was certain they could argue about this until the person on the other end of the phone arrived at the house and still not reach a consensus.

"Stop," Adelaide said, and Darius paused. She sighed. "If we do this, we have to do it smart. Kurt and

Sophie, it might be better if you stayed nearby, but you can wait outside for us if you'd rather. I'm staying here either way. Tetsu and Darius, you two can look, then tell us what you see. Be quiet and be slow. Got it?"

"We're not leaving you," Kurt said with a hint of a quaver in his voice.

"Fine," Sophie huffed. "We'll wait in the kitchen with you."

Darius grinned. Adelaide was even more impressive than he'd thought. He waited for Tetsu to join him at the basement door, then he eased it open. He was about to take a step when Tetsu shouldered past him.

"Me first," Tetsu hissed.

Darius stepped back and gestured at the staircase.

Tetsu's tennis shoes didn't make a sound as he lowered himself onto the first step, then the second. He eased himself down, stair by stair. They heard the man moving around the basement, but the bottom of the staircase remained clear.

Adelaide's eyebrows pinched together with worry as she listened at the top of the stairs. Darius wanted to reach out and smooth her forehead. He wondered what it would be like to kiss her. He forced himself to look back at the staircase, and as soon as there was space, he eased himself onto the first stair.

Darius and Tetsu inched forward. The lower portion of the staircase was framed in, but did not have any walls. A third of the way down the staircase, the two boys crouched down and peered through the gap into the room beyond. The pickle-like smell was stronger now.

The floor and walls were concrete, illuminated by fluorescent lights secured to the ceiling. Darius saw a long table covered with tools, surgical instruments and an open bottle of beer. Thick bundles of wire ran across the floor to where the man stood, his back turned, next to two gurneys. One was empty. A body lay on the other.

Darius craned his neck to get a better look. The body, half-covered with a white sheet, was adult-sized, but stitched together from different pieces. The skin on its arm was a different tone from its torso. The man moved and Darius could see the body's face. Its head was a different tone again. Darius grimaced as he realized a portion of the skull was gone.

The man positioned himself at the cadaver's head and probed at the exposed brain. The creature opened its mouth and let out a long, low groan. Tetsu shuddered. Darius felt his dinner shift in his stomach.

Darius and Tetsu locked eyes and retreated quietly

but quickly up the stairs.

"We have to go," Darius whispered to the rest of the group.

"What did you see?" Sophie hissed.

"Not here." Darius glanced at Tetsu and the two of them hurried everyone out of the house.

Six

The five friends stopped their bikes on a grassy knoll in the centre of the park. The area was cast in shadows, and the trees towered like strangers in the dark. Adelaide felt her blood pump through her veins. She'd never felt more alive.

Tetsu dropped his bike on the ground and paced in a small circle around the deserted park.

"What was down there?" Kurt huffed.

"Come on, what was it?" Sophie looked between Darius and Tetsu as she dropped her own bike.

"Give them a minute," Adelaide said. She'd never seen Tetsu act this way. She could see the faint light of the moon reflected off Darius' wide eyes.

"There was a body," Darius started.

"Not just a body!" Tetsu cut in. "It was a bunch of them, all stitched together!"

"Keep it down," Adelaide said evenly. She glanced around at the nearby houses.

"Keep it down? That guy is stitching bodies

together!" Tetsu snapped.

"Like Frankenstein?" Kurt asked.

Everyone looked between Tetsu and Darius.

"Yeah, he's making Frankenstein!" Tetsu's eyes darted around the park.

"He's ... never mind." Kurt shook his head.

"Tetsu." Adelaide put her hand on Tetsu's arm. "Tetsu, you're going to be okay."

"That was messed up," Tetsu replied. He took a deep breath.

"That isn't normal here?" Darius asked.

Everyone looked at him.

"Is that normal in Boston?" Adelaide asked.

"Well, no. But this place could be different."

There were rumours of strange happenings in Olympic Vista, but most people chalked them up to disgruntled Link employees and imaginative children. Adelaide, who wasn't one for gossip, remained quiet.

"Well, my dad says—" Kurt started.

"Your dad doesn't know shit," Tetsu interrupted.

"My dad says it's the commies," Kurt continued, ignoring Tetsu and leaning in toward Darius. "They're everywhere. They're at The Link. They conduct all sorts of experiments there."

"So, what do we do?" Sophie hissed in the darkness.

"We see who shows up to the house," Darius said. He sounded confident. "Then we can call the police."

"It's as good an idea as any," Adelaide agreed. "You guys don't have to come if you don't want to. We won't go back in the house."

They navigated their bikes back to Hyacinth Street in silence. They took refuge behind the long, low hedge of the yard across from the house they'd broken into. Adelaide guessed it must have been another twenty minutes before a dark van pulled onto the street.

"Is that blue?" Sophie whispered. "That's important for the police, right?"

"It's black," Tetsu replied.

"Keep it down," Adelaide urged.

The van pulled into the driveway of the dilapidated house. Two figures emerged, one from each side of the vehicle. It was too dark to make out their features, but one appeared to be male, the other female.

"What's he doing?" Sophie asked as the man walked to the back of the van.

"Shh," Darius warned.

"Why'd she go behind the house?" Sophie asked.

"To tell him they're here," Tetsu sounded irritated.

"What's in the van?" Sophie asked.

"What do you think?" Tetsu snapped.

"Shh!" Darius urged again as a light turned on in the house. "She's coming back."

The front door opened and the man from the basement stood in the entryway. The two newcomers removed a long black bag from the back of the van.

"That's—that's a body bag," Sophie gasped.

"What did you think they'd have?" Tetsu retorted.

The man held the bag, while the woman closed the rear van doors. Then the two of them carried the bag up to the front door. The man from the basement ushered them in. The woman let go of the body bag, and the man carried it through the doorway. She looked out toward the road. The light behind her illuminated her silhouette. The woman looked to be in her mid-thirties, short and curvy, her brown hair pulled into a ponytail. She shook her head and stepped into the house. The man from the basement peered out into the darkness before pulling the door closed behind them.

"Let's go call the police!" Sophie stood up.

"The police here are crap. A bunch of corrupt low-lifes who won't do shit about this," Tetsu gestured.

"Plus, we'd have to say we broke into the house,"

Kurt pointed out. "That's a crime, too."

"We have to do something," Sophie argued.

"If people are going missing, someone must be able to figure it out," Adelaide said. "Unless they collect people who are already deceased, people who then don't get to be buried." She didn't like the sound of that.

"We should get back, guys. My parents will kill me if they realize I'm gone," Kurt said.

"Are you going to be okay to get home alone?" Adelaide asked Darius. "We could all bike you back."

"I'll be okay. That's way out of your way. Thanks, though." Darius ran his hand through his hair.

"All right. If you're sure." Adelaide couldn't imagine cycling through the dark streets alone. She admired his bravery. "See you tomorrow."

"Yeah, you will," Darius replied as he turned his bike in the direction of his home.

"Bye, Darius," Sophie whispered into the darkness.

Then the group parted ways with Darius and cycled back to Pine Street.

Seven

The morning arrived earlier than Adelaide would have liked. She blinked, bleary-eyed, as she walked down the street. Beside her, Tetsu let loose with a loud, bottomless yawn. Kurt scurried down his driveway and joined them on the sidewalk.

"What's your mom's problem?" Tetsu nodded toward Kurt's house, where Agatha Zillman scowled out the window as Kurt fell in step with the others.

"She caught me out of bed last night," Kurt grimaced.

Adelaide looked up the driveway at the sad beige bungalow with a few planter boxes and no garden to speak of. It was a stark contrast to Sophie's house next door, which had freshly cut grass, well-manicured bushes, and several beds of colourful flowers. Adelaide knew Andy was the one who mowed it now. He'd started last summer. He was always focused on the task and her greetings were too quiet to be heard over the roar of the lawnmower.

Sophie walked down the front walkway of her yard

and joined the trio on the sidewalk. Together, they started toward the bus stop.

"Sophie! You forgot your lunch." Everyone turned as Sheila Katillion hurried down her front steps. She stood about as tall as her daughter, though her coiffed blond hair added the illusion of another inch of height. She wore a plain white blouse and jeans, and some light, natural-looking makeup. She presented Sophie with her pink plastic Strawberry Shortcake lunch box.

"Oh, thanks," Sophie muttered as she unzipped her bag and thrust it inside.

"You were almost asleep in your eggs this morning, Sophie." Sheila shook her head. "There's an extra slice for you as well, sweetie," she said to Adelaide as she handed her a wrapped package.

Sheila was one of Adelaide's favourite grown-ups, and it wasn't just because of the delicious snacks. She always seemed to display the right emotion for any situation. She was calm when warranted, but a cheerleader when someone needed one. In recent months, she'd begun to invite Adelaide to stay for dinner. Sheila always swore it was just because she'd made too much food, but Adelaide wasn't so sure.

"Thank you, Mrs. Katillion," she said. Her voice

remained flat, but the edges of her lips curled into the faintest of smiles, and Sheila beamed back.

"Well, have a great day, kids!" Sheila smiled at the lot of them, and Adelaide thought her gaze lingered on her for just a moment longer.

"What'd you get?" Tetsu asked.

"It's pizza," Sophie said.

"I like pizza. How come your mom doesn't give me any?" Tetsu grumbled.

"Probably because she feels bad that Adelaide—" Sophie stopped herself. "Maybe she doesn't like you."

Adelaide flushed.

"That's mean. And I'm charming." An impish grin stretched across Tetsu's face.

"Maybe she's just scared of your mother," Kurt offered.

"What do you think about Darius?" Sophie asked as they walked up the street to the bus stop.

"Oh, you're asking me," Adelaide fumbled as she realized Sophie's gaze was on her.

Sophie didn't wait for her reply. "I think he's brave. And fearless," she said, then scowled at the sky as small raindrops began to fall.

"Sounds like someone's got a crush," Tetsu teased.

"Bite me," Sophie huffed.

"Are we really not talking about last night?" Kurt asked.

"Hush," Adelaide urged. She looked around at the other kids at the bus stop.

The bus pulled up and they all climbed on. Adelaide settled into the seat second from the front and Tetsu sighed as he sat down next to her.

"You know, we're the cool kids now," Tetsu explained. "We don't have to sit at the front."

"I like it here." Adelaide settled into her seat. "You don't have to sit with me if you don't want to, though."

Tetsu slumped back into the seat as Kurt sat down one row behind him. Sophie moved several seats back and joined her friend Julie. Once everyone was seated, the doors closed and the bus continued its trek to James Morrison Elementary School. Tetsu and Adelaide sat in a comfortable silence.

***

"Hey, guys!" Darius ran up to greet his new friends as they got off the bus. He smiled at them, and his grin widened as he looked at Adelaide. She was dressed in jeans, a purple t-shirt and her jean jacket, with her wrist cuff on her right wrist. He admired how well she pulled it off.

"Hi, Darius." Adelaide's voice was monotone, but she smiled.

Darius' grin widened further. "Last night was crazy, huh? You guys did great. This place is great!" He ran his fingers through his hair.

"I still can't believe we stayed until the delivery came," marvelled Kurt. "Where do you think they got the body from?"

"It's better not to ask questions," Tetsu said sagely.

Darius frowned and shook his head. He had a lot of questions for Tetsu, but he was sure he wouldn't get any answers from him.

"I want to go back again, to keep an eye on the place," Darius said. He turned to Adelaide. "Want to join me?"

"I can try," Adelaide said. "I don't know how easy it will be for me to sneak out like that every night." She yawned. "It isn't quite as close to us as it is to you."

Even after the bell rang and everyone had filed inside and taken their seats, Darius couldn't stop grinning.

Eight

After school, Adelaide loitered near the pick-up/drop-off zone. Sophie had tried to convince her to try out for volleyball, but Adelaide had declined. The others had gone to the gym to watch, in the hopes Mrs. Katillion would give them a ride home later. The Katillions' blue minivan pulled into the parking lot and Sheila rolled down the window.

"Hi, sweetie! Did you want a ride?" she called.

Adelaide nodded and walked over. Her breath hitched as she realized there was a passenger in the front seat. She pulled the side door open. "Thank you, Mrs. Katillion."

"Hi, Adelaide," Andy squeaked. "Did you want some Chex Mix?" He twisted in his seat and offered a container out to her.

"Thanks, Andy," she smiled, as she climbed into the van and sat on the front bench. She reached over and took a handful of the mix. "How was school?"

"Oh, you know,"—Andy's voice went up an octave—"it's fine." He coughed.

"That's good." A hint of a smile played across Adelaide's lips.

"How is, um, how is it here?" Andy asked. He looked between Adelaide and the container in his hand.

"It's good." Adelaide admired his eyes. They were the sort of eyes she imagined people could get lost in.

"How's your mom?" Andy's voice squeaked again, but Adelaide pretended not to notice.

"Her boyfriend blinks too much," Adelaide said with a frown. She'd mentioned it to her mom, who had shrugged it off.

"He really does. I've seen him," Andy agreed.

"Really?" Adelaide's face relaxed and she gave Andy a soft smile.

"Maybe you should look into it, sweetie," Sheila suggested to her son. "You do want to be a detective."

Andy blushed.

A shiny black Lincoln Town Car pulled into the parking lot. Darius's dad stepped out. He looked at the school, then back down at his watch. His eyebrows knit together as he tapped his foot.

"Oh, my," Sheila murmured.

"That's Mr. Belcouer. His kids started here this year," Adelaide said as she took another handful of Chex Mix from the container. She imagined Andy as a detective in a long trench coat. He'd shake the hair out of his eyes before he reached for a notepad and a pen from his pocket. She wondered what he would have thought of last night.

"I had no idea he was back," Sheila mused absently.

"You know him?" Adelaide asked.

"Oh, yes. I used to go to parties at his house..." Sheila trailed off.

Adelaide cocked her head and opened her mouth to ask a question when the van door opened.

"Oh," Sophie muttered when she saw Adelaide. She glanced toward the front where her brother sat, then back at Adelaide. "You're getting a ride home, too?"

"How did it go, Sophie?" Sheila called from the front.

"It went fine," Sophie sighed. She gestured for Tetsu and Kurt to climb into the rearmost seat.

Sheila looked at her daughter in the rear-view mirror. "I'm glad, Sophie!"

Adelaide chuckled to herself. She enjoyed the way Mrs. Katillion refused to indulge Sophie's moods.

Adelaide watched as Drew Belcouer tapped his foot and stared at the school doors. As Tetsu, Kurt and Sophie clipped on their seatbelts, Davia strolled out of the school. Drew gestured to the car. Adelaide couldn't make out his words. Davia shrugged and walked to the car.

Sheila backed the minivan out of the stall. "Adelaide, did you want to come over for dinner tonight? I've made a meatloaf and there's plenty."

"Yes, please, Mrs. Katillion," Adelaide said as she avoided Sophie's glare.

Sheila put the van into drive and eased it forward. They had almost reached the Lincoln Town Car when it reversed suddenly. Sheila slammed on her brakes. Drew straightened out his car and pulled out of the lot onto the road.

"Is everyone okay?" Sheila asked. There was a chorus of confirmations. "The man drives like he owns the road," Sheila muttered.

"Technically the parking lot, Mrs. K," Tetsu pointed out. Sophie rolled her eyes.

***

Darius surveyed the house on Hyacinth Street. The

73

afternoon sun glinted off the windows of the nearby homes, but the dilapidated house was still and dark, and its boarded-up windows obscured the sun's rays. It was as if the house itself absorbed the light.

"Hey, kid!" a man called. Darius turned and assessed a rotund older man standing in the yard two houses down. "What are you doing loitering around here?"

"Nothing, sir." Darius walked toward him. "Do you know who lives there?"

"Ain't no one who lives there. Wish they'd sell the damn place. Actually thought they did once, but no one moved in." He looked at the house and shook his head. "Don't you get any ideas," the man said. "Trespassing is a crime whether someone lives there or not."

"I understand, sir. So, you never see anyone coming or going?" Darius pressed.

"It's empty. I know you kids like to dare each other to go in there, but it's just a house. Now get out of here. Go home to your parents."

"Thank you," Darius said.

He walked back to his bike and put the kickstand back up. He believed the man hadn't seen anyone, but that meant whoever the occupants were, they were being very careful.

***

"I'm sorry my brother got a ride back with us, guys," Sophie moaned over the top of Brian Wilson's croon. She flopped back in her favourite chair in the Hideout. "He is such a loser."

Tetsu wiggled back and forth on the blue bean-bag chair. Sophie winced at the noise. Adelaide focused on the chords of the Beach Boys' "Wouldn't It Be Nice" as they danced through the speakers.

"Andy's not that bad. You know, maybe everyone could be nicer," Kurt said.

Tetsu froze. Adelaide paused as she thumbed through the records. The song came to an end and amplified the silence.

"Pardon me?" Sophie raised her eyebrows.

"I just think it would be nice," Kurt mumbled. "He does live here, too."

The first notes of "You Still Believe in Me" eased the tension.

"Fine, I'm sorry, Kurt," Sophie sulked. "But you guys don't get it. You don't have a lame sibling that hovers around all the time."

"I've got my sister," Tetsu pointed out.

"So not the same. She's way older, plus she's cool. And she never tries to hang out with your friends," Sophie argued.

There was a knock at the door.

"I'm not coming in, but mom says your friends have to go. It's dinner time."

"See ya!" Tetsu said as he scooped up his bag. He glanced at the white and gold Corelle plate, which had been full of cookies when they arrived.

"Bye," Sophie said as she munched on the last one.

"You can have those anytime," Tetsu whined.

Sophie shrugged. Kurt scooped up his bag and everyone trundled up the stairs. Sophie and Adelaide waved goodbye to the boys, then washed up for dinner.

"Tough day at the salt mines," quipped Sophie and Andy's father, Jack, as he kissed Sheila's cheek. "Dinner smells great."

Sheila smiled, Sophie rolled her eyes, and Andy gave a half-smile. Adelaide felt warm inside. Jack made a crack about the salt mines every day, and Adelaide found the routine, and his deep voice, soothing. She wondered if that was how Andy would sound when he was a bit older.

"Hi, Adelaide. Nice to have you over. I understand Sophie joined the volleyball team today.

Did you?" Jack asked.

"Hello, Mr. Katillion. I didn't, no. Sophie said it's not fun."

"Well, it *is* work." Sophie nodded.

"That's what you said. If I'm going to spend my free time doing something that should be fun, I'd like to enjoy it. You didn't make it sound like I would," Adelaide explained. There was also the matter of the small fee to participate, but she didn't want to mention that.

Sophie sighed.

"Well, I suppose that *is* fair," Jack smiled. "How's your mom?"

"She's fine, thank you, Mr. Katillion." Adelaide passed the salad to Sophie.

"Well, that's great," Jack smiled.

Her mother had been in a great mood when Adelaide had checked in at home before coming to Sophie's. She was out of bed. And dressed. She had been busy coiffing her hair and applying layers of makeup for her date with Rico. Adelaide wondered what would happen if her mother was as dedicated to remaining employed as she was to keeping a boyfriend.

***

Darius breathed in the smell of cumin and hot peppers and sighed with contentment. He laid the white cloth napkin across his lap and folded his hands under the table.

"Thank you, Consuela." Miranda smiled at their cook.

"Si, it's my pleasure," the short, wiry woman answered as she set a dish down on the long table. Her hair was pulled into a tight bun, and her skin was leathery, as though she spent countless hours in the sun. Consuela had a severe face, but kind brown eyes. Darius had liked her the moment he met her.

"Elbows, Davia," Miranda prompted.

"Ugh," Davia sighed as she flopped her hands to her sides. She sniffed at the air. "What is this?"

"Chicken diablo, Miss Davia," Consuela answered.

Miranda smiled at Consuela again, then narrowed her eyes at Davia. "It smells wonderful."

"It should, for what we pay her," Drew murmured as Consuela returned to the kitchen.

"She isn't expensive. How was your day at the office?" Miranda asked.

"The new partners are idiots. We can't pay a cook what you suggested, Miranda," Drew argued as he served himself. "It's criminal. Like how long it took Davia to leave the school today. I won't stand for that. Make me wait again and you are off the team, do you understand?"

"Yes, Daddy, I'm sorry." Davia smiled and batted her eyes at her father.

"You're too old for that," he said as he glanced up. "And Darius, we won't have any problems like at the last school, will we?"

Darius could feel his father's gaze on him "No, Dad. Of course not." Darius forced himself not to shift in his seat lest his father think he was guilty of something. Darius knew he'd made a mistake in Boston, but he knew Davia broke more rules than he ever did. Darius wondered what, other than being caught, he'd done to earn his father's ire.

***

Adelaide watched Andy turn and head back up the street. She smiled to herself before she opened her front door. At Sheila's insistence, Andy always walked Adelaide home. The walk was short but comfortable and Adelaide savoured the time they spent together.

She stepped into the house, set her backpack on the

ground by the staircase, and slipped her shoes off.

There were wide double doors on each side of the entryway. To the right was the dining room, which was almost never used. Its doors were closed. To the left was the living room. Its doors were ajar and Adelaide could hear faint music drifting toward her. A dim light seeped into the hall.

Adelaide moved further into the house and opened the closet door next to the stairs. She tucked her shoes onto the rack and closed the door. She walked into the kitchen and put the leftover meatloaf from Sheila onto a shelf in the mustard-yellow fridge.

"Are you still here, Mama?" Adelaide called as she walked back into the front hallway.

"I'm here, baby," Belinda moped from the living room.

Adelaide stepped into the living room where her mother lay sprawled on the green tweed couch. "Don't Stop" by Fleetwood Mac played at low volume through the speakers. A half-eaten bag of chips was open on the table. The curtains were drawn and a single side lamp illuminated the room. The fireplace was cold and dark. The doors to the adjacent sunroom were pulled shut.

"He didn't call?" Adelaide asked.

"Nope. It's just us," Belinda replied as she looked up at her daughter.

"Did you eat?"

"Of course I did." Belinda gestured at the bag of chips.

"That's not dinner, Mama. Did you get groceries?"

Belinda made a pained expression. "I'm sorry, baby. I forgot."

Nine

"I've been back by that house a couple of times, but there's no sign of activity," Darius said, huddled outside the school with the others. Sophie wedged herself between Darius and Adelaide. The morning rain was heavy and most of the students were stuffed under any small amount of cover they could find.

"You shouldn't have gone alone. What if he snatched you?" Kurt asked as he stood next to Darius.

"I was fine," Darius assured him. He avoided Davia's gaze as she glared at him from near the door. She didn't appreciate their early arrival.

"Were the police there at all? Did you see?" Sophie asked.

"It just looked quiet, like I said."

"So, what are we going to do?" Sophie fussed. She moved an inch closer to Darius and bit her lip.

Darius couldn't tell how much of it was true concern and how much was an act. He shifted an inch away from her, toward Kurt. "I'll keep an eye on it this weekend.

Where's Julie?" Darius kept his tone as light as possible.

"She's sick today." Sophie smiled at him. "I'm free to spend time with you at lunch if you want."

"Oh, I…" Darius glanced at the others. Adelaide averted her gaze. "Well, yeah, you should hang out with all of us if you want."

Darius saw her try to hide her disappointment.

The bell rang and students pressed their way to the door. Students shoved past each other, eager to be out of the damp air. Adelaide was jostled from Darius' side and pushed out of the stream of students who funnelled into the school. Darius tried to stop but was propelled forward. He stepped to the side of the hallway and looked back. Brody, a large boy with chubby cheeks, slowed the students to a trickle and held the door open for Adelaide.

"Tetsu Nomura!" a teacher snapped.

Darius turned to see Mrs. Anders, a tall, severe-faced woman, in a nearby doorway. Her short dark blonde hair was streaked with grey. She wore a knee-length charcoal skirt and a white blouse.

"Don't push or it's straight to the office for you!" Mrs. Anders threatened.

"I wasn't …" Tetsu trailed off as he was jostled by another student.

"Don't you talk back to me," Mrs. Anders warned.

Adelaide navigated her way through the throng of students and stepped up next to Tetsu.

"We'll get to class now, Mrs. Anders," Adelaide assured her.

Darius fell in step with Tetsu and Adelaide. Mrs. Anders glowered at the lot of them as they continued down the hall.

"She always has it out for me," Tetsu grumbled.

"Why?" Darius asked. "What did you do?"

Tetsu turned and raised his eyebrows in a skeptical fashion. "Are you serious?"

"Yes." Darius looked between Adelaide and Tetsu. They'd reached the door to their classroom and Tetsu leaned in.

"It's because I'm Japanese," he whispered dramatically.

"Mrs. Anders has an issue with your family," Adelaide corrected Tetsu. "And it's not because you're Japanese."

"It's not *not* because I'm Japanese." Tetsu raised his eyebrows as if to challenge Adelaide's assessment.

"Let's just get to class." Adelaide shook her head and motioned at the classroom door.

Darius looked between the two of them. He had so

many questions, but the pair filed through the door and took their seats. Darius followed.

"Good morning, class!" Mr. McKenzie greeted the room.

Ten

Adelaide and Tetsu sat on the worn hardwood floor in her living room, eating cereal. Cartoon characters danced across the television screen in front of them. It was a long-established Saturday morning ritual.

"You, uh—" Adelaide pointed at Tetsu's chin.

"Thanks," Tetsu said as he wiped his chin with his arm. The milk left a faint streak across his skin. He shovelled another spoonful of cereal into his mouth.

"Mmhmm. You could slow down," Adelaide suggested.

"No way. I'm gonna have another bowl if I can." Tetsu grinned.

"A third one?" Adelaide shook her head as she fished the last of her Froot Loops out of her own bowl.

"Yeah! Hey, can't we turn the volume up? And why didn't your mom just use her bed?"

Adelaide had found Belinda asleep on the couch this morning before Tetsu arrived. She assumed her mother must have waited up for Rico, who hadn't bothered to show up. Adelaide had pulled a blanket over her and left her there.

"She was tired. These are still reruns." Adelaide gestured to the television where Papa Smurf lectured the other Smurfs on the importance of teamwork. Adelaide turned back to Tetsu. "I'm going to Rutledge's. Did you want to come?"

"Yeah, sure," Tetsu said as he shovelled the last spoonful of technicolour rings into his mouth. The bowl, which he held just under his chin, caught the milk that dribbled as he spoke.

Adelaide moved from the living room into the kitchen, where she inhaled the smell of freshly brewed coffee from the machine. She loved the smell, but thought the taste of coffee was horrible. She rinsed her bowl in the sink, then took Tetsu's and did the same. She'd wash them once she got back.

"Let's go," Adelaide said. She poured a cup of coffee for her mother and topped it up with sugar and milk. She set it down on the coffee table on her way out. She hoped that, with any luck, the caffeine would perk her mother up enough to look at the classifieds.

***

"Good morning, dear." Miranda smiled at Darius. She was dressed in her purple spandex leggings and teal spandex top with her robe pulled over. A plate of breakfast sat before her. Darius glanced at the grapefruit and small dish of yogurt. A basket of muffins sat in the middle of the table, but he knew his mom wouldn't touch them.

"Morning, Mom. Is Dad at the office already?" Darius asked.

"He certainly is," Miranda replied.

"It's our first Saturday in Olympic Vista and he's already working." Darius shook his head in fake dismay.

"Darius," Miranda warned, but her tone was light. Darius liked how she was when his father was absent. She was more playful and relaxed.

"I think Davia's still asleep. How was your workout?" Darius asked as he took a seat at the table. He smiled at his mother.

"Very good, thank you for asking." She beamed at Darius. She used a spoon to remove a segment of grapefruit and bring it to her mouth.

"Big plans for the day?" Darius asked.

"Very much, yes. The interior designer and the movers will stop by with some of the new pieces and take away some of the current furniture. I can't wait to see it go."

"Are we getting rid of it?" Darius asked, surprised. His parents had discussed new furniture when they arrived, but his father had spoken at length about how this was the family estate and how Darius' grandmother had had a large hand in its décor.

"No," Miranda sighed. "But at least I won't have to look at it. Your father will store it somewhere. What about you? Big plans?" she asked.

"Thought maybe I'd go for a swim," Darius said as he looked out the window at the overcast sky. "I understand we can use the pool now."

"It doesn't look nice out there," Miranda warned.

"You get wet in the pool anyway, Mom," Darius said. He picked up a napkin from the centre of the table, reached over to the basket and selected one of the oatmeal bran muffins Consuela had left for the weekend. He took a bite. It was moist and flavourful. He liked Consuela's cooking more than their chef's back in Boston.

In fact, he liked everything about this place more than Boston. His expulsion was the best thing that had ever happened to him.

***

Adelaide propped her bike against the wall of Rutledge's, then moved Tetsu's bike from where it lay abandoned in a parking stall. The sky was grey, like it so often was here.

"It's fine there." Tetsu waved his hand at his bike.

"Until it's not," she retorted.

The pair walked into the store and the bell on the door jingled. Adelaide sighed and set her lips in a grim line. The person behind the counter was a teenager in a polo shirt, not her favourite acne-faced cashier. The polo shirt cashier always kept his eyes on them and counted all of their penny candies. It was ironic because Adelaide was sure he was the store employee who had hidden those comics in the back the other day.

Tetsu loaded up a bag with penny candies. Adelaide selected a small handful and placed them in her own bag with the small plastic tweezers. She could feel the cashier's eyes burrow into her back. On the way to the checkout Adelaide picked up a newspaper. It was the real reason she'd come up here.

"You have to buy that before you read it," the cashier snapped.

Adelaide set the paper on the counter and handed over the bag of candy.

"There are fifty-three cents of candy there," Adelaide said in her monotone voice.

She fought the urge to roll her eyes as the teenage cashier moved each piece of candy around the bag. After a moment, he plunked the buttons on the till.

Adelaide handed over enough change to pay for her items, then stood aside for Tetsu to buy his candy. Again, the cashier shifted each piece of candy around in the clear bag until he was satisfied he had counted each one. After several moments, he punched a few buttons on the register.

"This stuff will rot your teeth," he said.

"That's what my mother says. Just ring it up, buddy." Tetsu scowled. He turned to Adelaide. "What are you buying a paper for?"

"My mom needs a new job."

Tetsu made a show of handing over the money to pay for his candy, then the two of them walked outside.

"That guy's an asshole. I hate him," Tetsu said as he looked around the parking lot for his bike.

"It's over here," Adelaide reminded him as she picked hers up. "I moved it, remember?"

"Right, but then how am I supposed to find it?"

***

A slight drizzle fell into the pool as Darius, on his back, lifted one arm above his head and pulled it through the water. He lifted his other arm and pulled it back down to his side as he swam the length of the pool. The water was cold, but pleasant.

For everything the Boston house had, a pool was not one of them.

One arm, then the other. Darius reached the edge of the pool, twisted his body, and began to swim back.

"Darius!" Davia called.

Darius glanced over, surprised he hadn't heard her arrive.

"What?" he asked without slowing his pace.

"I'm bored!"

"And I can help you how?" Darius asked. "Put on a swimsuit."

"It's rainy."

"You get wet in the pool," Darius retorted. He reached the edge of the pool once more, twisted, and began his return journey.

"It's not the same," she scoffed.

"So go do something," Darius suggested as his arms cut through the water.

"I can't! Daddy went into the office. Mom is refusing

to take me out in her car," Davia pouted. "Though it is kind of wasted if you can't have the top down."

"There must be something on TV," Darius tried.

"That's boring!"

Darius sighed. He knew there was no way to get rid of her. He stopped his backstroke and started to tread water. "How can I help, Davia?" he asked, giving her the opening he knew she was looking for.

Davia beamed at him. "Can you believe the kids here? I mean, they are so immature! I think that Farrah might have potential. I'm not so sure about the others. And you have to stop spending time with those losers. I mean, you'll drag down the family name, Darius."

Darius closed his eyes and sighed.

***

The light drizzle turned the pavement dark grey. Adelaide and Tetsu were on their bikes, some distance from their homes now. Tetsu struggled to keep pace with Adelaide, who channelled her frustration into movement.

"I don't see why you had to ask my mom why she needed the paper when I already told you," Adelaide fumed. She and Tetsu had returned to her house to drop off the newspaper. A wave of embarrassment crossed Belinda's face when Tetsu asked the question. Adelaide could still picture the hint of betrayal in her eyes.

Adelaide pedaled faster.

"I didn't hear you say anything about the paper," Tetsu argued, still struggling to ride next to her. "Besides, it was just a question. So what if your mom lost her job? Again."

Adelaide navigated her bike up Hyacinth Street and tried to put it out of her mind. She stopped across the street from the haunted house and surveyed it. It was daytime now, but the house looked the same with its boarded-up windows, unkempt yard, and empty driveway. A black car pulled up in front of the house. It was shiny and reminded her of Darius' father's car, but she thought it was a bit smaller. She wasn't good with cars.

Two men stepped out. Each of them wore a suit and sunglasses. They looked at each other, then walked up the driveway to the front of the house.

"So are you not talking to me now?" Tetsu asked.

"Shh," Adelaide hushed him as she moved her bike up the road. "Come on."

"Yeah, no, I see them. I think it's weird, but are you mad at me? 'Cause you've been mostly quiet since we left your house, and that was a while ago."

"Shh," Adelaide repeated. "Yes, I'm mad. You never listen."

"Well, gosh, maybe if you didn't speak like a robot all the time you'd be more interesting to listen to."

Adelaide swivelled her head and stared at him. It was as though she'd been punched in the gut. She could feel cracks form in the protective wall she'd built around herself.

Tetsu cast his eyes down and cringed. "Adelaide, I'm real sorry, I didn't mean—"

"Stop," Adelaide said. She hopped on her bike and pedaled away before he could see her blink back tears.

***

Darius spent an hour on a self-guided tour of the town. He still didn't know what was where, and hadn't known where to look, but he enjoyed Davia's absence. He'd humoured her as long as he could, but when she wouldn't stop making fun of Adelaide and her friends, he'd had enough. He'd invited his sister along for a bike ride, knowing full well she would have no interest. Darius enjoyed the solitude as he meandered down various roads as the whim struck him. He was about to turn home when he noticed someone cycling toward him.

"Adelaide?" He grinned as they crossed paths. "Hey, are you okay?"

"I'm fine," she said, but it looked like she was trying not to cry.

"What brings you out my way?" Darius asked. While he hadn't known her long, Adelaide always seemed stoic. He wanted to know what was wrong, but he didn't want to push it.

"I thought I'd check out the haunted house. There's activity there now, but—"

"Really? Let's go! Come on!" Darius started to pedal and looked back to make sure Adelaide was right behind him. She was.

Minutes later they dropped their bikes at the end of the road and walked up Hyacinth Street. They found Tetsu lurking in the bushes on the property across the road from the house. Darius could almost smell the guilt radiating from Tetsu and he wondered what had happened between the two of them.

Tetsu refused to meet Darius' gaze.

"There, see?" Adelaide pointed at the black sedan parked on the street in front of the dilapidated house.

"No one's come out," Tetsu offered.

"What are they doing? How many of them were there?" Darius asked. He looked between Adelaide and Tetsu.

"Two. Both in suits. With sunglasses," Adelaide said. Her voice was still flat, but he noticed she refused to look at Tetsu.

"Okay, come on," Darius said as he looked around. He wanted to help them, but if Frank Hardy had taught him anything, it was that time was of the essence when solving a mystery. He reached into his pocket and pulled out two bobby pins. He hoped he could pull it off. "Keep a look out, okay?"

"Okay. What are you going to do?" Adelaide whispered back.

"Find out who they are." Darius grinned as he moved toward the driver's side of the car.

"This is a bad idea," Tetsu said to Darius.

"Then stay here." Darius shrugged as he slinked closer to the car.

"Do you even know what you're doing?" Tetsu hissed.

Darius ignored him as he looked around. He couldn't see any sign of movement. He crouched down by the car and bit his lip as he inserted the first pin at a right angle and put the curled side into the lock. Then he inserted the second bobby pin right into the lock, less than an inch deep. He held the first one still and moved the second one around inside the lock.

"Adelaide," Tetsu warned as she scanned the area. "This is a bad idea."

"Shh," Darius hushed him. He wasn't sure if Tetsu could hear him, but it made him feel a bit better. He grimaced, took a breath and moved the second bobby pin around again. Then he heard it click. He grinned and eased the door open. The car smelled of stale cigarettes.

Darius knew he needed to check the glove box. He kept low in the seats as he reached over and depressed the button. The small door fell open.

"Barkly?" Adelaide sobbed. "Barkly, where are you?"

Darius froze.

Eleven

"Barkly?" Adelaide sobbed again. Darius glanced through the passenger window. Adelaide moved closer to the dilapidated house and positioned herself in the driveway, between the approaching men and their car.

"Everything okay?" a male voice asked.

"No, no," Adelaide wailed. "It's my dog, it's Barkly. I can't," she heaved, "I can't find him. And I need him."

Darius ducked back down as he caught a glimpse of the two men. He reached over and pulled the vehicle registration out. Darius scanned the document. The car was registered to a Gary Stevens. Darius pushed himself further into the car.

"What does he look like?" the male voice asked.

"He's brown and about yay high. He has big happy eyes and he's always wagging his tail." Adelaide sniffed. "I love him so much."

"When was the last time you saw him?" the voice asked.

"Who cares? Let's get going," the second man said.

99

The driver's side door pressed against Darius' calves. His hand touched something cold and metal. His eyes widened at the snub-nosed revolver tucked inside the glove compartment.

"No! Please," sobbed Adelaide. She took a step toward the house. "Barkly. Do you two live here? Have you seen him?"

"Live here?" chuckled the second man. The men turned so they still faced her. Their backs were to the car now. "No, we . . ." He paused. "came to check the structural integrity."

Darius withdrew his hand from the glove compartment and slid back across the seat. The emergency brake dug into his stomach as he tried to keep low.

"Did you hang posters?" the first man suggested.

"I, I haven't," Adelaide sniffed. "That's a good idea. Where would I make those?"

Darius lowered himself into a crouch and pulled himself out of the car. He was about to close the door when he noticed a plastic card on the lip between the seat and the doorframe. It had a magnetic stripe like his father's credit card. He flipped it over. It was an ID card.

"The print shop, kid," the second man said. Darius heard the scrape of a lighter igniting. "Look, get out of here. We've got stuff to do, and you shouldn't loiter around a run-down old building like this one." He paused. "You ever go in there?"

Darius pocketed the ID card. He shifted his weight and shuffled away from the vehicle. His heart pounded in his chest as he held his breath, pushed down the lock, and eased the door closed behind him. The door caught, but it didn't close all the way. Darius gave it a soft bump with his hip. The car jostled and Darius held his breath. The door fell flush with the rest of the car.

"In there? That looks dangerous," Adelaide gasped. "Unless—did you see Barkly in there?" Her voice quavered.

"No. No dog. Hit the print shop," the second man directed.

Darius scrambled back to the bushes across the street. His heart pounded in his chest.

"You could've gotten her hurt," Tetsu hissed at him.

Darius could see Adelaide across the street with the two men. They were both middle-aged, dark-haired, and dressed in slacks and sport jackets. One took a drag on the cigarette he held between the first two fingers of his right hand. The other was shorter with a slightly round belly.

Adelaide used her arm to wipe away a tear from

her cheek. The man with the cigarette took another long drag as he moved away from her and rounded the car. He unlocked and opened the driver's side door. The other locks popped open and the short man climbed in the passenger side. Once they were both inside the car, they drove up the road.

Despite their appearance, Darius felt the two of them were as mundane as the rest of the small town. He had already learned enough to know not everything was as it seemed.

Adelaide stood still and watched until they were out of sight, then she strode across the road.

"Did you get anything?" she asked in her usual deadpan voice.

"That was awesome! You were amazing!" Darius gushed. "Who is Barkly?"

"My made-up dog," Adelaide said with a shrug. "We didn't talk about *how* I was supposed to keep a look out. I improvised."

"We are going to go far, you and me!" Darius grinned.

"What was that? You could have been hurt!" Tetsu scowled at Adelaide.

"I was fine. I can take care of myself," Adelaide spat.

Darius surveyed them. The two were friends, of that he had no doubt, but Tetsu reminded Darius of some of the entitled bullies he knew back in Boston. He forced himself to take a breath and keep his hands relaxed. In the short time he'd known Adelaide, he'd noticed that she alternated between an impassive face and a look of concern where her eyebrows pinched together. Whatever this was, it was new. There was fire in her eyes.

"Go home, Tetsu," Darius ordered. "You're being mean to my friend."

Tetsu turned and appraised him. Darius pulled his shoulders back and stood up as tall as he could. He wasn't much taller than Tetsu, but he made himself as imposing as possible.

Tetsu moved his jaw to the side, and looked over at Adelaide. He shook his head, picked up his bike and cycled down the street without another word.

"I got a card." Darius turned to Adelaide and held it up. "Want to see if we can get into their building?"

Twelve

"No way!" Darius gasped as they stopped their bikes at a nondescript, single-storey building. It had several frosted glass doors, some labelled with the names of various businesses. Archie's Bookkeeping and West Coast Electronic Repair were on either side of an unmarked frosted door. A single black car was parked in the small parking lot.

"That can't be them," Adelaide marvelled.

"Same car," Darius pointed out. "It has the same license plate."

Adelaide had gone with Darius back to his house after Tetsu had left. The card Darius had stolen identified the cigarette-smoking man as Gary Stevens, a National Park Service agent. They'd looked in the phone book for National Park Service, but hadn't found a branch in Olympic Vista.

Darius had offered to bike Adelaide home, and she'd agreed. Instead of going straight to her house, though, Adelaide had taken a detour. She'd wanted to prolong her visit with Darius, but it seemed she'd accomplished more than just that.

"What are the odds?" she wondered aloud.

"Hurry!" Darius pointed to the side of the building and the two of them scrambled behind it as the two men from earlier emerged from the unmarked door. They walked to the car, climbed in, and drove off.

"Wait," Adelaide hissed as Darius stepped out of the alley. "You don't want them to see you in the rear-view." He ducked back into the shadows of the building and waited until the car was out of sight.

The two of them made their way to the unmarked glass door. Darius pulled the card he'd taken from the car out of his pocket. A small device protruded from the door frame halfway up the door. Darius ran the card through it. The light flashed green and the door disengaged with a click.

Darius turned to her and grinned. "Thanks, Gary. Let's go!"

Adelaide nodded and followed him through the door into an entry area, where a poster of Smokey Bear insisted only they could stop forest fires. The entrance opened to a hallway on the right. Along one wall was a series of numbered mailboxes, each with a keyhole. At the end of the corridor was a single closed door.

The two picked their way down the carpeted hall. A clock in the entrance ticked as the second hand moved around the clock. Adelaide listened for any sign of movement in the room at the end of the hall. Unable to hear anything, she reached for the door handle, grimaced, and pushed it open.

The room, which was illuminated by a fluorescent light, smelled of stale coffee and cigarette smoke. The floor was covered in blue checkered linoleum. Four heavy wooden desks were in the centre of the room. Typewriters sat on three of them, while a computer sat on the fourth. A long countertop with a coffee machine ran along the wall just inside the door. The machine itself was off, but a series of thick rings of old coffee rimmed the carafe. Large grey metal filing cabinets lined most of the opposite wall.

Darius walked to a door on the left-hand side of the room and twisted the handle.

"Locked." Darius shook his head.

"Maybe there's a key," Adelaide murmured as she opened the desk drawers. She found a set of keys in short order. There were several smaller keys on the ring, as well as a larger one that opened the door.

The next room was the size of a closet, and was

filled with banks of monitors. A fan whirred on the ceiling above them, but the air in here still felt warmer. The screens each had a different display. One was of the front entrance, another the bank of mailboxes. One showed the exterior of the entrance, and one was of a room full of filing cabinets. One displayed an unfamiliar corridor, and another a well-appointed office. A single screen was turned off, and the office area they'd been in was not visible on the monitors.

"Look at that one." Darius pointed to a monitor that displayed what Adelaide guessed was a cell.

Movement in the corner of her eye caught Adelaide's attention and she turned to look at one of the other monitors. There was movement at the entrance. Adelaide watched on the screen as the front door opened. She wheeled back to face the larger room they'd come in from.

The front door banged closed. Adelaide looked at the desks and the cabinets beneath the countertop for somewhere to hide. Seeing nothing, she stayed in the closet room and pulled the door closed.

Footsteps drew closer, and then light from the other room seeped under the door and illuminated the floor. Adelaide stepped back, right into Darius. The two were pressed against each other and the warm monitors. She could hear his breath. He smelled of sandalwood and pine.

***

"It has to be here somewhere," Gary Stevens said as he searched the office drawers.

"Why would it be in a drawer? You weren't even in one of them."

"It has to be somewhere, Ray." Gary slammed a drawer closed.

"You should keep it in your bag. Or your wallet."

"That's not helpful right now," Gary growled. "Why don't you help me look for it?"

"That house was messed up." Ray peered into the garbage can.

"We should put two in his chest and one in his head." Gary looked up from the drawers. "That's not looking."

"We were told to stand down," Ray reminded him. He nudged the garbage can with his foot and peered at the floor behind it. "And I am looking."

"I don't agree."

"It doesn't matter if you agree. We do what we're

told. That's the point of the defense industry," Ray argued.

"What if it's in the sub-basement?" Gary asked.

"Why would it be in the sub-basement? You didn't go down there today."

"We should check it," Gary proposed.

"If we access it today, it'll trigger a report. That'll be worse. I won't let you get me in trouble for this, Gary. You should report the card."

"I'm not reporting the card. Keep your mouth shut about it. It'll turn up," Gary growled. He pulled a pack of cigarettes out the interior pocket of his sport coat and tapped one out. "It's not here. I hope it's not in that damn house."

***

The light turned off, and the footsteps receded. Adelaide's heart beat fast in her chest. She breathed in sandalwood and pine. She had Darius' hand in hers. She wasn't sure if she had taken his, or him hers, while the men rummaged through the office, but neither had let go.

Adelaide turned her body so she faced Darius. They were mere inches from each other, almost pressed together. He was illuminated by the light from the monitors. One half of his face was cast in shadow. His eyes were wild and hungry, like a child who'd awoken Christmas morning to find a room filled with presents, doodads, and a bright shiny bike.

She closed the gap between them and pressed her lips to his. His lips were soft and warm. Darius leaned forward and kissed her back.

"I, um, think they're gone now," Adelaide said as she pulled back a moment later. She cast her eyes over the monitors, then looked back up at him.

"That was nice," Darius grinned.

Adelaide smiled and nodded in agreement. With his hand still in hers, Adelaide eased the door to the office open.

"All clear." She led him out. "What do you think the sub-basement is?"

"Maybe where that cell is? That office too?" Darius guessed.

"I still want to know what's in the mailboxes. Think these keys will work?"

"Oh, yeah!" Darius nodded. "Let's go."

They crept into the hallway, and found a key that fit the lock on the top corner of the bank of mailboxes. There were twelve boxes in total. There were envelopes in three of them, and one contained a small box. Adelaide withdrew an envelope, slipped her finger into the small opening, and ripped it open.

"That looks like a dossier," Darius declared.

The name "Grover Jergen" was typed onto the top piece of paper in the envelope. It also contained his last known address, phone number and date of birth.

"He worked at The Link." Adelaide pointed. A quick scan of the rest of the documents revealed Grover Jergen had developed a prototype method for birds to communicate with people through speech. It was reported to have amplified their intelligence, but there were instances of heightened aggression. The work had been terminated last year, but the research and Grover Jergen had disappeared two months ago.

"This guy," Darius said, as he gestured at the mailbox the envelope had come from, "is supposed to find Grover Jergen?"

"And eliminate him if he's trouble," Adelaide said. She pointed at one of the pages. "He's also supposed to bring back the technology. Let me get a new envelope, we'll put it back."

"They'll kill him!"

"Maybe, but they've already issued the orders. If we

don't put it back, they'll figure it out, and reissue them. Plus, they'll find out what happened to the first ones." Adelaide gestured toward the room with the monitors. "I don't know how to delete the recordings, do you?"

"No. Fair point. I want to know what the others say though." Darius looked at the other mailboxes with curiosity.

"Me too, but what if they come back to search here again? His card is here, after all," Adelaide pointed out.

Adelaide searched the office, found a new envelope to replace the one they'd opened, and used one of the typewriters to relabel it. The pair locked everything back up and replaced the keys.

"You have to leave it," Adelaide said, gesturing to the key card in Darius' hand.

"I know." Darius pursed his lips in frustration. "But I, I mean, we could…" Darius glanced at the bank of mailboxes.

Adelaide put her hand on his arm. "It's time to go."

Darius nodded and dropped the key card next to the wastebin by the door.

Thirteen

"I didn't know you could mix flavours," Adelaide said, marvelling at her chocolate cherry milkshake.

As Darius had observed, Adelaide's face seemed to always be either impassive or full of worry, and right now it looked decidedly worried. He wanted to smooth down her eyebrows and kiss her. He'd been surprised when she'd kissed him. He hadn't been ready to let her go home after they'd left the National Park Service office, so he'd suggested they get a bite to eat.

They sat at the diner, which Adelaide had assured him was the best place in town to get food, other than Oceanside Pizzeria. She'd admitted when they arrived that it was also one of the only other places to get food in town that wasn't at the mall.

The red booths were well-worn. The floor was a checkerboard of black and white tiles. Fake plants lined the deep windowsill that looked out into the half-full parking lot. The place smelled of French fries and burgers. Patsy Cline twanged from the red and baby-blue jukebox.

"Sometimes you just have to ask," Darius said with a shrug. "Live dangerously."

Adelaide smiled at him. His heart skipped a beat. Darius wanted to be her boyfriend more than he'd wanted anything else in his life.

"You and Tetsu, are you two... are you his girlfriend?" Darius asked.

Adelaide's eyes bulged and she laughed. Darius had never heard her be so loud. A middle-aged couple at a nearby table turned and looked at them. The woman smiled. Adelaide clapped her hand over her mouth. Darius wished he could listen to her laugh forever.

"No. I'm not Tetsu's girlfriend."

"No? I thought maybe..." Darius trailed off. He ran his hand through his hair.

"Tetsu and I have been best friends since kindergarten. But no, I don't have a boyfriend. Dating anyone seems stupid." She leaned over and took a sip of the milkshake.

"Oh." Darius tried to hide his disappointment.

The waitress, who was dressed in a frilly blue apron, dropped two orders of burgers and fries off at their table.

"Thank you," Adelaide said to the waitress. "And thank you," she added to Darius.

"My pleasure!" Darius smiled at her.

"I don't know when you arrived in town, but there was an incident at Pine Park a couple of weeks back. Late August," Adelaide recalled in her monotone voice. She picked up the ketchup, opened it, and tapped the bottom of the glass bottle until some poured onto her plate. "A flock of angry birds attacked a bunch of people. They actually closed the park for a bit."

"You think it's connected to Grover Jergen and his aggressive birds?" Darius asked. He picked up his burger to take a bite, then stopped and held it a few inches off the plate.

"Probably. Do you think we should warn him?" Adelaide asked. She picked up a fry and swirled it in the ketchup before she lifted it to her lips.

"There must be something we've missed," Darius mused. "I still don't understand why government agents wouldn't just try to arrest him. I can't imagine why a guy obsessed with birds is so dangerous that they'd have to eliminate him."

A wave of concern rippled across Adelaide's face. "I hope he's not that dangerous."

"Honestly? I just don't know where we'd even start to look for him." Darius grimaced.

Adelaide nodded in agreement.

Darius took a bite of his burger and grinned. The food was as good as Adelaide said it would be.

"Tell me more about The Link," Darius coaxed.

Adelaide popped a fry into her mouth and tilted her head to study him. She chewed the fry with an impassive look on her face.

"What do you think I know?" she asked after a moment.

"More than me, I'm sure. Kurt said it's full of commies. That can't be true, though."

"How do you know?" Adelaide asked.

"It just can't be."

"It could be, but I doubt it is," Adelaide said as she swirled a fry in ketchup. "I don't know how much you know, but it's a research facility of some sort. This place used to be just forest with a bit of farmland. Back in the fifties, this guy James Morrison—that's who our school was named after—visited the area. He thought it was a good fit for his science stuff." Adelaide put the fry in her mouth and chewed.

"Science stuff? Like what?" Darius asked.

"I don't know, really. Some people say he researched really out-there stuff. Other dimensions. Aliens. Super advanced robots. Someone in town said, 'If you can think of it, The Link does it.' I don't know how much truth there is to it." Adelaide's eyebrows furrowed. "Or, at least, I didn't."

"Researched?" Darius asked. He was confused by her use of the past tense, as he'd heard The Link was still open.

"I heard he died a few years ago. Of course, by then lots of other people had moved to town to work for him." Adelaide shrugged.

"Who runs it now?" Darius' mind raced. "Is the haunted house a part of it? What about those men? Do you think any of them work for The Link? How is it all connected? What other weird things happen here?"

"That's a lot of questions." Adelaide picked up another fry, swirled it in ketchup and popped it into her mouth. She was quiet while she chewed it.

"And why is it called The Link?" Darius asked.

"Everyone calls it The Link. There was an article in the paper with Mr. Morrison a bunch of years ago. He said something about how we are all linked, or lots of places are linked or…" Adelaide paused. She eyed her burger but picked up another fry instead. "Honestly, I'm not even sure anyone remembers exactly, but everyone started calling the place The Link after that. Sometimes you might see vans out with the word MALTA on them. That's them. It's the Morrison… Astro-something… Laboratory of Technical Advancement, or something like that."

"Is Morrison still in charge? What about the haunted house?" Darius asked.

"I'm not really the best person to ask." Adelaide looked apologetic. "I didn't pay close attention before. I think it's a nephew or a son or something? And I have no idea how the house is connected."

"But we could find out?" Darius asked.

"I don't see why not," Adelaide answered. "But that's a job for a different day, and right now I want to eat this burger."

"Oh, I'm sorry!" Darius hadn't realized all of his questions had prevented the two of them from eating.

"It's okay," Adelaide assured him. She gave him a small smile across the table. Darius grinned back. In less time than he would have liked, the two of them had finished their food and biked back to Adelaide's.

"This is me." Adelaide gestured to the large old house at the end of the street.

It was a three-floor house, though Darius guessed

there was room for a basement. There were a few empty planter boxes, the grass was a bit long, and the front steps sagged. The large front porch was devoid of furniture or potted plants. The house looked old and tired.

It reminded Darius of a forgotten relic with stories to share, if one would only stop and listen. Even more than the house itself, the expanse of trees behind the property drew his attention. The trees were a thick tapestry of shades of green.

"You have a forest?" Darius gaped.

"Yes. Well, no." Adelaide frowned. "I mean, it isn't ours. Anyone can go there. But we have access off the backyard. Everyone else has to find one of the public trails."

"That's so rad." Darius grinned.

"I guess." Adelaide shrugged as she turned toward the house. "It's just always been that way." She hesitated, then turned back to face him. "We could check it out sometime. If you wanted."

Darius forced himself not to grin any wider. "I'll talk to my dad and see when I can come over."

Fourteen

Adelaide sat on the long bench at the wooden banquette in her kitchen. She surveyed the dark green linoleum floor and made a mental note to sweep it when she got home after school. The countertop was a mess as well. She suspected someone had decided to have a late-night snack and hadn't bothered to clean up. Toast crumbs dusted the countertop and there was a smear of jam on the white cabinets. She'd have to clean that up as well.

She heard footsteps from the hall and sighed.

"Good morning," Rico said as he stepped into the room. His smile didn't reach his eyes. He blinked rapidly at Adelaide before he turned and reached into the mustard-yellow fridge. He pulled out a container of orange juice and let the door swing shut.

"Hello," Adelaide said. She took a bite of her Rice Krispies.

"You should be nicer to me, you know." Rico blinked some more as he opened the container.

"What do you mean?" Adelaide asked. She looked

down at her bowl. It was almost empty.

"You should be nicer to me." Rico's eyelids flapped like birds trying to take flight.

Adelaide hated when adults told her how to be. Talk more. Smile more. Talk less. Be more excited. Be quieter. Be nicer. Be more like a kid.

Rico took a swig of orange juice out of the carton.

"I'm not sure I'm not nice to you," Adelaide frowned, and took another bite of cereal. She made a mental note not to drink the orange juice.

"You could be nicer. I am your dad now." Rico chuckled. It was a strange noise and it set Adelaide on edge. Her frown deepened.

Adelaide lifted her bowl and drank back the last of the cereal and milk. Without a word she rinsed the bowl and collected her backpack. She could feel Rico's eyes on her. She looked over and he continued to blink rapidly, a big fake smile plastered across his face.

Tetsu's knock sounded at the front door. As much as Adelaide didn't want to see him either, he was a welcome relief.

"Bye, Rico." Adelaide pulled her backpack over her shoulder and walked out of the kitchen. She glanced up the staircase as she made her way through the foyer.

Adelaide suspected her mother was still asleep. She and Rico had been up most of the night. Adelaide opened the door and stepped outside. She looked at Tetsu, then turned, locked the door behind her and headed toward the bus stop.

"How was the rest of your weekend?" Tetsu asked.

Adelaide heaved a sigh and looked at him. She was still annoyed with him.

"Look, forget what I said, all right?" Tetsu said. His eyes were pained, but he spoke with his usual bravado.

Adelaide took a deep breath, and began to speak with an unusual cadence to her voice. "It must be *awful* to have to be *friends* with someone people could mistake for a robot." She gestured in an animated fashion with her hands to embellish her words. "I don't want that for *you,* no, I don't!"

Sophie stepped out of her house. Her hair was larger than usual, and her eyelids were painted blue. She smoothed her acid-wash denim skirt as she approached the others.

"Oh *wow,* is that a new *skirt?*" Adelaide asked as she continued to emphasize her words with an exaggerated enthusiasm.

"Why is she talking like that?" Sophie stopped in her tracks.

"I upset her." Tetsu cringed.

"I'm *totally* fine," Adelaide said with a wave. "If Tetsu likes me better like this, then we,"—she pointed at him—"are all,"—she pointed again—"good! It looks *great* on you, Sophie."

"Fix it!" Sophie cried.

"I don't know how!" Tetsu turned on Sophie. "Did you remember your lunch?"

"Yes! But fix her!" Sophie squawked. She turned back to Adelaide. "Do you really think it looks good? Or is this just because of how you're talking?"

"It. Looks. *Fab!*" Adelaide beamed at Sophie.

Sophie moaned.

"Hey, Kurt," Adelaide said in a quiet monotone as Kurt fell in stride with them. He looked haggard.

"Hey," he replied.

"Everything okay?" she asked with a concerned frown.

Kurt closed his eyes for a moment and nodded. "My dad was just in a bad mood last night."

"Adelaide, what did Tetsu say to you?" Sophie demanded.

"It's *fiiine*," Adelaide drawled as she turned back to the others. "He just said I sounded like a *robot* all the time.

123

But *now*," she smiled, "I *don't!*"

"Tetsu." Kurt shook his head. "I like the way you speak just fine, Adelaide." Kurt smiled at her and she squeezed his arm in return. Adelaide wished there was something she could do for him.

The four of them made their way to the bus stop.

"So? How was *your*,"—Adelaide pointed at Tetsu and continued with her dramatic voice—"weekend?"

"Come on, Adelaide, please," Tetsu begged.

***

Darius was unable to think of anything but Adelaide all weekend. He knew Tetsu had upset her, but he still didn't know how. He waited near the front of the school and approached her when she stepped off the bus.

"Did Tetsu make things right with you?" Darius asked Adelaide, who shook her head. Darius looked at Tetsu. "I'm not okay with you until Adelaide is. You're a mouthy kid who treats people like garbage."

Tetsu recoiled and blinked. Darius turned back to Adelaide and studied her to make sure he hadn't gone too far. Her face was impassive as she looked at Tetsu, then walked on toward the front doors of the school. Darius followed. Kurt paused for a moment, then scurried after them.

"I've been thinking about the neighbour who saw me the other day," said Darius. "I think we should go back and draw his attention."

"Get him to call in some suspicious activity at the house. I like it." Adelaide nodded. Her voice was the same even monotone. He found it soothing to listen to.

***

Adelaide breathed a sigh of relief as Darius came into view. She'd biked along the quiet streets alone and hadn't liked it.

"Hey!" Darius grinned at her. His white teeth reflected the light from her flashlight taped to her handlebars. "That's pretty clever." Darius pointed at the light. He had noticed Adelaide's make-shift headlight, but she didn't feel any judgement. Instead, she got the impression he approved of her creative solution.

"Thanks," Adelaide said. "Make do with what you have, right?"

"For sure," Darius said as he turned the light off on his bike and pulled a flashlight from his bag. "So we can make a quicker getaway." Darius handed her the first flashlight and pulled out a second one for himself. "You won't have to reattach your headlight. Ready for this?"

Adelaide nodded and wondered if he ever had to make do with what he had. She turned her makeshift headlight off and the pair set their bikes down, pointed in the direction of the road for an easy getaway. The house, which was almost familiar now, was quiet. They walked up to one of the front windows.

"Here," Darius said. "We start here." He turned his flashlight toward a house across the street and down, and focused it on the windows.

"Do you think it's strong enough?" Adelaide asked. She focused her beam in the same direction.

"I don't know."

After a moment, Darius fished a pry bar out of his bag.

"I suppose we shouldn't be quiet about this." Adelaide looked around and wondered if there was any chance they'd be caught. Her heart pounded in her chest.

"Not really, no. But we have to be ready to run." Darius paused and looked at her. His face was serious and he held her gaze. "Adelaide, if that guy comes out here you run to your bike and you go. Don't wait for me, just go."

"I won't leave you here."

"Adelaide—"

Adelaide leaned forward and kissed him. "For luck."

***

Darius grinned as Adelaide pulled away. Her lips were soft. He wondered what it would be like to kiss her for longer.

"We should…" Adelaide gestured at the house.

Darius nodded and forced himself to focus. He pushed the pry bar into the space between the plywood and the far window of the house at one of the corners.

Adelaide cleared her throat. When she spoke she adjusted her tone just as she had for her Barkly story a few days prior. "Do you think we can get in there?" Adelaide called. Her voice was loud in the dark.

"Of course we can!" Darius called back, trying to make his voice deeper than usual. He adjusted his grip and pulled on the prybar. He could feel the board shift as the nail loosened.

"That's it, you can do it," Adelaide urged more quietly. She flashed her beam of light at the window of the nosy neighbour.

The board shifted.

"That's one down!" Darius called in an exaggerated fashion.

He moved to another corner and repeated the procedure. Adelaide looked between the neighbouring houses and this one.

"Still no sign of activity," she reported. Darius popped a third corner free. "Oh, there."

A light turned on at the house they'd flashed their lights into.

"Help me." Darius directed her to the board. Together the two of them removed the piece of plywood from the window and dropped it on the ground. It made a soft thump as it landed on the overgrown grass.

"We have to get the window open as well," Adelaide said.

Darius nodded. He peered into the window, and wondered if the mad scientist had heard them. He slid the prybar into the window frame.

"That's another light over there," Adelaide said as another window lit up at the neighbour's house.

"Almost," Darius grunted, "there!" The window opened the slightest bit.

The two of them pushed it open further.

"We're not going back in, are we?" Adelaide looked at Darius.

"I think we have to. Otherwise, the nosy neighbour will think he scared us away."

Adelaide nodded. "Then the police might not go in. Okay." She flashed the light in her hand across the lawn in a dramatic fashion and then redirected the beam into the now open window.

"You'll be right behind me?" Adelaide asked.

"I can go first," Darius offered.

"No, I've got this," Adelaide said. Her usual monotone was touched with a hint of a smile and Darius grinned in the dark. Adelaide took a breath and climbed up onto the window ledge and into the room. "Come on, then."

Darius' grin widened as he pulled himself through the window and into the house. They moved their beams around the room. Unlike the room full of furniture they'd climbed into last time, this room was completely empty. Motes of dust floated through the air and reminded Darius of the glitter in one of his mother's Christmas snow globes.

Adelaide approached the closed door that led to the hallway. As she reached for the handle, an audible thump echoed out from the otherwise still house. They both froze.

"It's just that boot," Darius said with a chuckle. His heart pounded in his throat. "Here," Darius offered as he stepped forward and reached for the door handle. His hand grazed Adelaide's and he jumped as a small static shock discharged.

Adelaide let out a small snort of a chuckle.

"Ready?" Darius asked.

Adelaide turned back toward the window and shone her flashlight out into the night. "Ready," she said as she turned back to the door.

Darius swung the door open and looked out into the hall. It was as still and empty as he remembered from their previous visit. The flashlight stretched down the long dark hallway. Then it flickered and went out.

Darius hit the side of it once, and then once more. It flickered again, then went dark. He shoved it into his back pocket.

Somewhere deep in the house, a chain rattled. Another thump.

Adelaide sucked her breath in. Darius ran a hand through his hair. As he dropped his hand back to his side, Adelaide caught it. Her skin was soft and he wrapped his hand around hers.

"We've got this," he said. His voice sounded confident, but inside his stomach butterflies flapped with reckless abandon.

"I know," Adelaide said. She shone her flashlight down the hall. "Come on."

The two of them crept down the hall hand in hand. Adelaide paused at the closed door of the room with all the furniture.

"Hang on," she whispered as she opened the door. She pulled Darius inside and picked her way across the cluttered room to the window. Satisfied, she redirected her beam of light toward the door. They stepped back out into the hallway and moved toward the main entry. A floorboard creaked under Darius' foot and he drew his breath in with a small hiss.

He navigated them toward the staircase and the two of them picked their way up the steps. Adelaide aimed the beam of light just a few steps ahead of them as they ascended the staircase.

A footstep sounded above them. Darius hesitated for a moment, then took another step.

"Just the machine, right?" Adelaide asked. Her voice was almost inaudible. "We'll just shine the light out the upper windows?"

"That's right," Darius whispered back. He didn't let go of her hand as they reached the hallway upstairs. Together they crept along the hallway to the first door on the left. With his free hand, Darius turned the handle and pushed the door open.

The contraption in the attic thumped the boot into the floor again and the pair tensed. They stepped into the room. Heavy beige curtains were drawn across the window, but the room was otherwise empty.

"Come on," Darius whispered as he led Adelaide across the room. The floorboards creaked under their weight. Darius reached out and pulled the curtain back. The upper floor windows weren't covered in plywood and Darius looked out through the dirty window onto the street.

"Lights are still on, that's good. Here, give me the flashlight for a second."

Adelaide handed Darius the flashlight and turned to look behind them as another footstep sounded from the attic.

Darius shone the flashlight beam out between the boards, then down at the floor, and then up through the window once more.

There was another footstep. Adelaide stiffened beside him.

"Darius," she hissed. Her hand squeezed his. "That one wasn't from upstairs."

Darius felt his heart beat in his throat. He cast the flashlight beam about the room and it settled on a wooden closet door. He pulled Adelaide with him across the room and sucked in his breath as he opened the closet. It opened without a sound. The flashlight illuminated the small empty space. Adelaide stepped through the doorway and Darius moved in behind her. He pulled the door closed, and turned off the flashlight.

Fifteen

Footsteps ascended the staircase. Thump. Thump. Thump.

Adelaide's heart beat so loud in her ears she wondered if Darius could hear it. The footsteps reached the second floor. She tightened her grip on Darius' hand. The footsteps drew closer. Adelaide sucked in her breath.

When Adelaide was six, her mother had rented a room out to a man with long blond hair. He always smelled of tobacco. When adults were around, the man had a large agreeable smile.

One morning, while her mother was still sleeping off a late night, Adelaide put on the album *Baby Now That I've Found You*. She smiled when the needle scratched the record. She loved the static just before the music began to play. Then the music started. It was just loud enough for her to sing and dance along. She'd been twirling around the living room in her rainbow striped skirt to "Build Me Up Buttercup" when the blond man stomped down the stairs. His eyes looked like they were on fire. She'd frozen in place, one arm still up in the air.

She'd learned to be quieter after that.

Tucked inside the closet of the haunted house on Hyacinth Street, Adelaide closed her eyes and focused on her breathing: in, then out. In, then out.

The footsteps moved down the hallway toward them. Adelaide flinched as the door to the room they were in was flung open. It hit the wall with an audible bang. Light seeped in under the closet door as the light in the room turned on. Adelaide's heart beat in her ears.

There was another thump as the door across the hall was flung open.

"If you're up here, I'll find you!" the man from the basement called.

There were more footfalls as another door was flung open.

"Adelaide," Darius hissed in the darkness. "We have to make a break for it."

Adelaide nodded, then realized he couldn't see her. "Okay," she whispered.

"On three," Darius whispered back. "One." He squeezed her hand.

Another door down the hall was flung open.

"Two."

"Where are you?" the man called.

"Three!" Darius hissed. He pushed open the closet door.

Adelaide blinked as her eyes adjusted to the light. She let Darius drag her from the closet. They rounded the corner into the hall. The hall light had also been turned on. Adelaide looked up the corridor and saw a man in a lab coat. Even from where they were, she could smell something that reminded her of pickles.

"Come on!" Darius urged.

Adelaide forced herself to look away and the two of them charged down the steps. The light from the upper hallway dimly illuminated the stairwell.

"Get back here!" the man yelled.

Adelaide and Darius reached the middle landing and rounded the corner to descend the final half of the staircase. Darius stumbled on a step and Adelaide tightened her grip on his hand. He righted himself and the pair sprinted on.

They could hear the man's steps as he charged down the hall and began his own descent down the stairs.

The lower floor was dark, as it had been when they'd arrived. Darius turned on the flashlight and the beam of light skipped over the wooden boards as he ran.

Darius headed for the front room they had come in through, but Adelaide pulled him into the back room full of furniture.

"This way! The window we used last time. That way the neighbour won't see us leave," she hissed.

They scrambled over a rolled-up rug and around a pile of side tables that had been stacked atop each other. Adelaide let go of Darius' hand and reached for the window.

It sounded like the man was at the bottom of the steps now.

She grabbed hold of the wooden frame and pushed it upward, but it held fast. Darius reached over with his free hand.

"Come on," Adelaide whispered.

The man's heavy footfalls pounded down the hallway. Adelaide and Darius strained against the window. Adelaide glanced behind her as a shadow darkened the doorway, then she blinked as her eyes were flooded with light. She couldn't quite make out the man's features in the newly illuminated room.

"Adelaide," Darius urged.

Adelaide shook her head and turned back to the window. She pushed upward hard and with Darius' help, the window opened an inch.

"Got you!" the man yelled from the doorway of the room.

Adelaide put her fingers through the small opening and grasped at the bottom of the window. She shoved the window upward and it banged into the frame above it.

The man strode forward. Adelaide hesitated.

"Go!" Darius yelled. He grabbed at the piece of plywood outside the window, which still hung from a single nail. He tossed his flashlight out the window and held the board to the side.

Adelaide pulled herself up into the window frame and started to climb out of the house.

She heard the man push his way through the room as a small side table clattered to the floor.

Adelaide glanced behind her. The man was only feet from her and his long arm reached out. Her breath caught in her throat.

Darius twisted to the side and put himself between Adelaide and the man. She heard Darius grunt as the man grabbed him and his fingers wrapped around his shirt.

"Just go!" Darius called as he strained against the man's grasp.

"You're not going anywhere!" the man yelled.

The man jerked Darius back from the window. Darius lost his grip on the plywood. Adelaide jumped the rest of the way out of the window and the plywood hit her leg as it swung back into place.

"Darius!" Adelaide called.

She turned and grabbed at the plywood. Inside, Darius squirmed and tried to writhe free of the man's grasp. Adelaide cast about for some way to help. Her eyes met Darius'.

"Go!" he called again.

Adelaide looked at the ground around her. Her eyes fell on the flashlight Darius had tossed out. She scrambled to pick it up, then ran back to the window, moving the plywood back out of the way with her left hand. In the light of the room, she could see panic on Darius' face. He strained and pulled himself along the floor toward the window while the man struggled to stay on top of him. Adelaide sucked in her breath, raised the flashlight in her right hand, and threw it straight at the man. It sailed through the air and clubbed him on the side of the head.

"Shit!" the man yelled. He staggered back and clapped a hand to his head.

Darius scrambled to his feet.

"Come on!" Adelaide hissed.

Darius scurried for the windowsill. Adelaide held the plywood back. Darius climbed out and dropped to the ground, and Adelaide let the plywood swung back into place behind him.

"Get back here, you little shits!" the man yelled from the window. He pushed at the plywood and tried to lift a leg out through the window.

Adelaide glanced at Darius and the two of them ran. They reached their bikes and, without a word, climbed on and pedaled away into the night.

Sixteen

The next day, Darius sat impatiently at his desk at school. He was so excited he vibrated. He was desperate to get back to Hyacinth Street and see what had happened after they left. He sighed with relief when the bell rang. He couldn't believe it was only lunchtime.

As soon as people finished their lunch and the second bell rang, Darius pulled on his teal windbreaker and fell in step with Adelaide as they headed outside. The sky was clouded over and raindrops dotted the ground. It was cooler today than it had been the last few days, and Darius zipped up his jacket.

Tetsu wandered off on his own, dejected. Darius watched with relief as Sophie ran off to meet some other girls. He looked around for Kurt, but couldn't see him. He liked Kurt.

"I don't know how you're so awake," Adelaide said. She was dressed in jeans, her jean jacket and a black t-shirt with the words "Fury Fire Blaze" written on it.

"Me neither. I just am. I really want to get back

there. As soon as I get home, I'll take my bike out there. Can I call you? Once I see what's happening, I mean."

"Okay." Adelaide's voice was almost devoid of tone. She yawned and covered her mouth with her hand. "I want to know." She smiled at him. The two of them walked around the schoolyard.

"Your shirt, what is that?" Darius asked as he pointed.

Adelaide looked down at her shirt as though she'd forgotten what was dressed in. "Oh this, right. Fury Fire Blaze was the band of one of our old roommates. They broke up, but the shirt is comfortable."

"It's a rad shirt." Darius' heart beat faster in his chest. He thought about their kiss at the house and the one at the office. "So, that, uh, I mean, when you..." Darius trailed off.

"When I ...?" Adelaide asked.

"When you," Darius leaned in and whispered, "kissed me."

"Oh. That. Sorry about that." Adelaide surveyed the playground and avoided his eye contact.

"Don't be sorry," Darius gushed. "Don't be sorry at all. I liked it."

"Okay." Adelaide nodded. Her face was as solemn as ever.

"I was just wondering, I mean, what brought that on?"

"I was nervous and excited I suppose." Adelaide shrugged. "I appreciate you not telling anyone."

Darius' heart dropped.

"Hi, Darius!" a few of the girls called as he and Adelaide passed them.

"Hi," Darius said. He gave them a small wave and turned his attention back to Adelaide. There was a chorus of giggles. Darius tried not to grimace at the noise. He liked the way Adelaide had laughed with her whole body at the diner.

"Darius?" Adelaide asked.

"Yeah?" Darius turned and looked at her.

"Maybe your dad could give me a ride and I could come over straight after school. We could go look at the house together. I wouldn't have my bike, but we could double."

All Darius could do was grin.

***

Adelaide balanced on the back of Darius' bike as he pedaled down the street. They were close to Hyacinth Street. Her hands tightened on his shoulders as he rounded the corner. The day had passed at a snail's pace after last night's excitement. All day she'd wished she could have a nap, but now she felt more awake than ever as the property came into view.

There was police tape around the ramshackle house; two squad cars were parked in front. Darius biked up the driveway of the house across the street and two of them tucked themselves behind the hedges. The view was better in the daylight than it had been on their previous visit.

Two officers emerged from the house.

"No sign of who the sicko was?" one officer asked the other.

"Not our problem. Let that new detective deal with it," the second officer chuckled.

"I've never seen anything like that." The first officer shook his head. "Who pieces together bodies in a basement?"

"Frankenstein?" suggested the second officer. "Who cares? Our shift is over. The coroner's got the body now."

"Isn't it bod*ies*?" the first officer argued.

"I don't know." The second officer grimaced. "All stitched together, it was like one body. I'm getting a drink."

"Aren't you curious?" the first officer asked.

"Not really. No." The second officer sighed. "Leave it with that detective. She creeps me out and I want to get out of here." He motioned to the car.

"The detective is what creeps you out? Not the…?" The first officer gestured at the house.

"Just get in the car," the second officer insisted.

The first officer glanced back at the house and shook his head in disbelief while the second climbed into the driver's seat of their squad car.

"We did it." Darius grinned.

"I guess we did. Whoever that guy was, he can't do that there anymore. Still, I'd feel better if they'd found him." Adelaide frowned.

"They should," Darius assured her. "They will."

A shiny black car pulled onto the street. The first officer glanced up at it, but climbed into the police cruiser. Adelaide recognized the black car immediately. She crouched lower behind the bushes and peered out through a small gap in the branches. The car slowed as it passed the house. Two familiar faces looked out the car window at the scene. Then the car sped up and drove on.

"That was them, wasn't it?" Darius asked.

"Yes. If they are government agents, why didn't they stop?" Adelaide asked.

"Maybe they aren't what they seem?" Darius suggested.

"That's bad. They did say they were there about building integrity. Do you think they could be secret agents?" Adelaide mused.

Darius grinned at her. "I don't know, but it sounds like another mystery to me."

Adelaide smiled.

Darius motioned to his bike and the pair rode off, wondering what other mysteries they could unearth in Olympic Vista.

Olympic Vista Chronicles

Life is good, if mundane, in Olympic Vista. Twelve-year-old Adelaide Winter and her friends spend most of their time biking around or hanging out in the Pacific Northwest town. Crushes, troubles at home, and the latest music or comic book release are their biggest concerns. Sure, there are rumblings of what happens at the secure research and development facility locals call The Link, but the adults about town assure the children there is nothing to worry about. And adults never lie, do they?

Darius Belcouer's arrival in the summer of 1986 changes everything. Together with their friends, Darius and Adelaide are determined to figure out exactly what the small town is hiding.

Book One: *Yesterday's Gone*
Book Two: *Songs from the Wood*
Book Three: *Costumes & Copiers*
Book Four: *Farmhouse Fiasco* (coming spring 2022)

Preview of Book 2:
Songs from the Wood

Amidst the cacophony of jeers, laughter and friendly banter, the silence in the front most bench of the school bus was deafening. It was early morning and the front lawns and gardens sparkled with morning dew. The school year had only recently begun and most of the students were still excited for the potential the next ten months held. The pleasant-faced driver pulled the yellow school bus onto the side of the road and opened the door to let the final batch of students climb aboard.

Adelaide tucked her long brown hair behind her ear as she stared out the window. Her black leather wrist cuff, which was studded with black and white squares, peeked out from the cuff of her denim jacket. She wore her usual solemn expression as she admired a garden alive with echinacea. Adelaide had no idea what the pink flower was called, but she wondered how it would look in her own yard. Once the new arrivals were safely seated, the bus continued its trek down the streets of Olympic Vista toward James Morrison Elementary School.

"Won't you talk to me? Normally?" Tetsu begged.

He sat slumped in the seat beside Adelaide. Behind him, their friend Kurt shook his head, amused.

"Isn't this *normal?*" Adelaide asked with a strange cadence to her voice. She plastered a fake smile across her face before she turned and looked at her best friend. A few days ago, Tetsu had suggested Adelaide's usual monotone voice made her sound like a robot. While she'd heard similar comments from people in the past, his words wounded her and she wasn't ready to forgive him. "It is," she paused for emphasis, "what *you* wanted. Isn't *it?*"

Tetsu slumped further into his seat. "It really isn't."

The clear sky had already started to cloud over as the bus pulled up to its usual spot outside the sprawling, one story, beige building. A large white sign with black letters spelled out James Morrison Elementary School.

Students collected their bags and pushed their way to the exit as the bus doors opened. Adelaide, who preferred a seat at the front of the bus, was one of the first students off. She left without looking at Tetsu and made her way toward the covered area of the school grounds.

"Adelaide!" Julie called as she exited the bus a few people behind Adelaide. Like most of the girls in their grade, Julie wore vibrant skirts and matching tops. Today she was dressed in a bright pink skirt and sweatshirt.

Julie didn't live in Adelaide's neighbourhood. She boarded the bus several stops prior to Adelaide's stop. Sophie, who did live on the same street at Adelaide, often sat with Julie on the bus. While Sophie often spent time with Adelaide, Tetsu and Kurt outside of school, she had dedicated this year to being popular. Popularity did not follow Kurt or Tetsu around, but today it seemed to follow Adelaide.

Adelaide stopped and turned. Julie and Sophie approached her. The two girls walked in step with each other and Adelaide tried not to frown.

"I'm so excited about this weekend. I think your mom is just the best! Will that cool guy with the cowboy hat be there?" Julie prattled.

"Waylon?" Adelaide's brow furrowed. "He's our roommate."

"It's so cool that you have roommates." Julie flicked her crimped brown hair over her shoulder.

"Okay," Adelaide said confused. "When will he be where?"

Julie giggled in response.

Adelaide gritted her teeth at the noise. She turned and searched Sophie's face, but Sophie refused to meet her gaze. Tetsu and Kurt stepped in next to the three girls.

Julie turned as the shiny black Lincoln Town Car pulled into the parking lot. Everyone else's gaze followed. They watched as Davia Belcouer climbed out of the passenger's side. Her butter yellow blouse, which had lacy frills down the front, was tucked into her jeans. She wore shiny black shoes and a pair of socks that matched her top. Her long blond hair was coiffed like the models in the latest issue of *Teen Beat*. She slung a jean jacket over her shoulder and closed the car door.

While everyone else stared at Davia's exit from the car, Adelaide's gaze fell on Darius., who got out of the back seat. Davia and her older twin brother had moved from Boston with their parents at the end of the summer. Both of them had a faint Boston accent, but that seemed to be where their similarities ceased. Where Davia strived to be popular, Darius was more determined to have fun and explore the strangeness of Olympic Vista. A smile played at Adelaide's lips as she recalled sneaking out of her house to investigate a so-called haunted house at Darius' suggestion. The entire adventure had left the group with more questions than answers.

Darius' eyes were wide and hungry for excitement as he looked about the schoolyard. They made Adelaide yearn for something she couldn't quite describe. She flushed and looked down at the ground as he caught sight of her.

"I love her clothes," Julie murmured.

Sophie sighed and rolled her eyes.

Although Davia was new to the school this year, she had already proved herself to be one of the most popular girls at James Morrison Elementary School, much to Sophie's dismay. Last night Adelaide, Kurt and Tetsu had listened to Sophie lament about Davia in the Hideout, a room in the basement of Sophie's house.

Adelaide looked up as Darius made his way across the parking lot toward them. He gave her a big wave and an even bigger grin.

"She killed a person, you know," Tetsu said. His words interrupted everyone's thoughts.

"What?" Julie gasped as they all turned to look at him.

"Davia. She killed a person, but she's too young and rich to go to jail." He nodded knowingly.

"Yeah, that's true." Sophie followed Tetsu's lead.

"I have to warn people," Julie gulped. She turned and ran off to another group of students nearby.

"That was mean," Adelaide said in her usual monotone voice.

Tetsu shrugged. The four of them watched as Davia approached Farrah Turner, last year's most popular female sixth grader. Farrah's blond hair had also been teased and sprayed to perfection. Today she wore her rhinestone jean jacket. If the most popular girl this year wasn't Davia, it would be Farrah.

***

Darius grinned at Adelaide as he joined the circle of friends in front of the school. Adelaide's lips curved slightly and offered a small smile back.

"What's going on guys?" Darius asked.

"Tetsu is up to no good," Adelaide said in her deadpan voice.

Darius frowned at Tetsu.

"Come on," Sophie interjected. She tilted her head to the side with an imploring look at Adelaide. "That was funny."

"Only until it catches up with you both," Adelaide warned them. She turned to Darius. "Want to walk?" Adelaide asked. "You can come too, Kurt."

Kurt brushed his reddish-brown hair out his eyes and looked between Adelaide and Darius, and Sophie and

Tetsu. Darius smiled at him. Of all of Adelaide's friends, Kurt was his favorite. He reminded Darius of Quinton, a boy from Wiltshire Preparatory Academy back in Boston. The two hadn't been friends exactly, but Darius had stepped in when classmates bullied him.

"See you guys," Kurt said to Sophie and Tetsu as he fell in step with Darius and Adelaide.

Darius hadn't been able to stop thinking about the house he, Adelaide and the rest of the group had investigated last week. As far as they could tell, a mad scientist or two had attempted to make their own Frankenstein's monster in the basement of an otherwise deserted house. After Darius and his new friends drew attention to the building, the authorities had intervened.

Darius had kept an eye on the paper ever since, but there had been no mention of an arrest or the incident itself. If the authorities covered up the dead bodies in basements, Darius reasoned there were even more mysteries in the small town to unravel.

"Maybe we should look into the bird man," Darius proposed. He was desperate to find something else to look into. His breath hitched as he recalled how alive he'd felt when he looked into the haunted house. Adelaide had seemed as invested as he was. And they'd held hands under the table in the kitchen. He wanted to spend more time with her.

"Grover Jergen?" Adelaide asked. "I don't even know where we'd start."

"We could check other newspapers for signs of aggressive birds outside of Olympic Vista. Maybe he's gone further afield. Or we could try to track down his family," Darius suggested.

"Good ideas." Adelaide nodded. "But if those agents we saw at the house are on the look out for him, we probably won't get to him before they do."

"I still can't believe you two broke into a government building and looked at secret documents." Kurt shook his head. "I'm afraid Adelaide is probably right, though. I suspect they have vaster resources than either of you."

Darius turned and smiled at Kurt. "You really do read a lot, don't you?"

Kurt's cheeks turned a light red. "I guess so," he mumbled.

"Sorry, Kurt. I didn't mean to embarrass you. It's a good thing," Darius assured him. He thought about the envelope he and Adelaide had found inside the office building and about all the other information that must be stored inside those walls. He desperately wished he still had the key card he'd stolen from the agent's car, but he knew Adelaide had been right to make him leave it behind in the office building.

The bell rang and they filed inside.

***

It was mid-morning and Adelaide's classmates fidgeted in their desks. Their teacher, Mr. McKenzie, had been reviewing the multiplication tables and very few students enjoyed it.

Adelaide's stomach rumbled. She hoped no one noticed. Her mother had forgotten to get groceries again and the brown banana and stale rice cake Adelaide scavenged for breakfast hadn't done much to fill her stomach.

"And just before recess, let's talk current events," Mr. McKenzie said to the class. "As you all know, I encourage you to read the newspaper. It's important to be aware of what's going on. Can anyone give me some examples of things going on right now?"

A girl named Heather put up her hand.

"Yes, Heather?" Mr. McKenzie asked.

Adelaide thought she detected a hint of surprise

in his tone.

"Whitney Houston won at the MTV music awards," Heather offered.

"That is current events. Thank you, Heather. Anyone else?" Mr. McKenzie asked.

The room filled with silence.

"Alright, well, for example, it looks like some local flocks of birds are becoming increasingly territorial. Do any of you recall when Pine Park closed late this summer for a short time?"

A few people put up their hands, Adelaide included. She sensed Darius, who was often attentive in class, sit up straighter.

"Very good! You followed the news." Mr. McKenzie smiled.

"No," Brody said. "My neighbour told me about it. A bird snatched a whole apple right out of her hand. She screamed really loud when it flapped in her face. Made me glad I stayed home and played video games all summer." Brody wore a grim smile.

"And thank you for that, Brody." Mr. McKenzie smiled a tight smile and nodded. "Fresh air is good for you, but I'm glad you weren't the victim of a fowl mugging at the park."

Mr. McKenzie paused for dramatic effect. "Anyone? No?"

Adelaide chuckled quietly to herself. Mr. McKenzie winked at her.

"Alright then." Mr. McKenzie opened his mouth to carry on when another student put his hand up. "Yes?" Mr. McKenzie asked as he nodded in the student's direction.

"That's not exactly current though, Mr. McKenzie," Reggie pointed out.

"Thank you, Reggie. I'm getting there. It seems there was another similar incident just outside Seattle." The bell rang and students shoved their books into their desks. "Take it how you will, students. I'm not sure if we should put out bird feeders to placate them or just be wary. Go! Enjoy your recess." He waved them to freedom.

"We could stay inside and play video games," Brody suggested. "That would be safer."

"Video games can't be the solution to everything, Brody." Mr. McKenzie chuckled. "Off you go!"

Adelaide felt bad for Brody. He was a bulky kid, the kind of boy who would either grow into his size or forever be called names by his peers. Brody had sausage fingers and chubby cheeks, and his short-cropped hair made his head look too big for his body. He smelled vaguely of meatloaf and body odour.

Brody didn't have a lot of friends and so last year Adelaide had taken care to be extra nice to him. She'd greeted him before school and said goodbye at the end of the day. She'd been rewarded with her initials next to his. According to several people who sat next to him, Brody doodled "AW + BT" all over his notebooks and surrounded them with a heart.

Adelaide hadn't said anything about it, but it made her uncomfortable and she hadn't been quite as friendly to him since.

Running shoes squeaked against the floor as the students migrated to the playground and field. There was the usual hum of conversation, but Adelaide's attention was on Darius. He walked alongside her and she caught a whiff of pine and sandalwood, which she'd come to associate with him. Adelaide inhaled through her nose and savored the smell.

"I bet it's Grover Jergen!" Darius exclaimed. "I didn't see the article because I only looked at the local paper." He grimaced. "I should have looked at other papers."

Adelaide nodded. She suspected Darius was correct, but she wasn't sure how they could go investigate in Seattle.

"Maybe Farrah will be at the party," Tetsu teased Kurt as they passed through the school doors and spilled out onto the school grounds. "You could kiss her." Tetsu puckered his lips.

"Shut up," Kurt mumbled. He looked down at the ground and kicked a rock.

"What's this party everyone is talking about?" Darius asked.

"Yes, what is this party?" Adelaide echoed. She had almost forgotten her conversation with Julie earlier.

"Sophie told everyone you're having one." Tetsu shrugged. "I figured you knew. Part of this new you you've got going on."

Adelaide's hands turned clammy. A shiver ran down her spine and her vision started to blur. She felt like the world was being pulled out from under her feet and there was nothing to grab onto.

Dear Reader

Thank you for reading this book.

The Olympic Vista Chronicles are a labour of love and have been published by me as an independent publisher. What does that mean? It means that I have decided to publish this book myself, for myself (and you!) rather than sending it to a publishing company that would help me get my books to you. I'm an independent publisher or an 'indie' author. Sounds cool, right? All authors rely on their readers, but indie authors like me especially depend on their devoted fan base. (That's you, I hope!)

If you enjoy this book, I would love it if you would tell a friend, write a review, or pick up the next book in the Olympic Vista Chronicles series! You can also join me on social media or sign up for my newsletter (I'll even say thanks by giving you a free short story).

Thank you again. I literally couldn't do it without you!

Kelly Pawlik lives on Vancouver Island, BC with her husband, their three inquisitive children, and two lazy cats.

You can follow Kelly on:
Facebook: kellypawlikauthor
Instagram: kellypawlikauthor
TikTok: @kellypawlikauthor
Twitter: @KellyPawlik84

Visit her website at olympicvistapublishing.com

Sign up to receive Kelly's newsletter and get access to sneak peeks of upcoming novellas, behind the scenes information and other exclusive content. You'll also recieve a free digital copy of "Snow Day," an Olympic Vista Chronicles short story right away!

Manufactured by Amazon.ca
Bolton, ON

25629575R00094